INSERTION

WILBUR
McKESSON

ISBN: 978-0-578-35497-2 (Hardcover)
ISBN: 978-0-578-35552-8 (eBook)

Any references to historical events, real people, or real places
are used fictitiously. Names, characters, and places
are products of the author's imagination.

Front cover image © Shutterstock.com
Book design by theBookDesigners

First printed edition 2022

Published by Wilbur McKesson
www.authorwilburmckessoniii.com

I dedicate this book to my father, Wilbur Andrew McKesson, Jr., who preached that character is the most important attribute in life. Your character is the only thing that follows you wherever you go, never leaves you, and is the only thing people will remember you for.

Rest In Peace

PROLOGUE

The C-130 Hercules reached its maximum ceiling for the early morning HALO jump at thirty-five-thousand feet. Jumping into extremely hostile situations behind enemy lines was one of the Bering Group's specialties. All six members of the Bering Group trudged to the ramp lowering at the back of the plane. They admired the astounding view of the curvature of the Earth as they waited for the green light to jump. After this, their month-long stint of being stationed covertly in South America would be over.

The light in the cabin turned green, and the team—dressed in neoprene suits, new state-of-the-art full-face helmets, and tactical equipment—fell forward, dropping like a stack of dominoes into the brisk air above the canopy of the Colombian jungle.

After ten minutes of falling, their boots touched the ground. They dropped their flight suits, wrapped them inside of their parachutes, added some rocks, and sunk them in the river nearby. Outfitting their gear, loading their weapons, and checking their earpieces, the team trekked four miles to the objective until they were twenty-five yards outside the small compound. By the time they reached their destination, it was just over eight-thirty in the morning—but with the dense canopy, you couldn't tell.

Jack Knowles knelt next to a *Euterpe precatoria* tree and marveled at its large leaves and ability to block the sunlight from reaching the ground. The humidity was unbearable. He closed his eyes for quick relief, thanking himself for bringing more water than usual. He was getting too old for this. He gently grabbed the bill of his withered Washington Nationals baseball cap and placed it on the dirt next to him. His team knelt with their back toward him in a 180-degree formation, their weapons raised and ready to shoot. The old days of Ops-core helmets with lapel microphones attached were gone, at least for them. It was baseball caps and throat microphones, easier to use and less sweaty when trekking through the jungle.

"Ben, do you see anything?"

Ben Williamson sat in the back of the C-130, cruising overhead. After all, he wasn't hired for his hand-to-hand combat skills. Tracking the team with thermal imaging via the satellite made it easy to see through the canopy and play overwatch.

"Everything looks good," Ben said. "Good luck, boys, I'll be here if you need me."

Jack nodded in silence along with the rest of the members. "Okay, boys, slow is smooth, smooth is fast." All five men acknowledged, creeping toward the tents. In the time it took the rest of the team to get into position, Nate, the precision marksman, climbed thirty feet into a *Euterpe precatoria* tree nearby to find a perfect spot overlooking the compound. The team wasn't going to move until he gave the final go-ahead.

"Team two, checking in," Jack said, as Kyle and Alex sat crouched behind him right outside their tent.

"Team one, checking in," Kwame whispered. He and Pete were kneeling on the opposite side of the compound next to the far tent.

"Roger," Nate whispered, looking through his scope. "Both teams standby. Team one, hold, there's two armed guards with AK's standing next to team two's entrance."

"Do you have a clear shot?" Jack asked. His right thumb nudging the selector lever off safe. His Springfield Armory Saint short barreled rifle was ready to speak clear instructions to anyone on the other end of the silencer attached to it.

"Yes, standby," Nate said, slowing his breathing down enough to accurately control his shot. He placed his gloved right finger on the trigger and, pulling it toward him, he felt the recoil of the rifle move through his body. He quickly transitioned to the second target. Both rounds hit their mark. "Tangos down, all teams execute."

Lifting his rifle, Jack felt Kyle's hand squeeze his left shoulder. Jack noticed out of the corner of his eye Kwame and Pete rounding the corner of their tent seventy yards away and lining up at the entrance. With his rifle lowered just below eyesight, Jack felt the hand of Kyle once more, giving him the go-ahead to make entry. Grabbing the tarp with his left hand and keeping a firm grasp of his rifle with his right, he entered the tent and took the path of least resistance. All men cleared their sectors of fire as their muzzles met in the center of the tent.

Nothing but beds lined both walls, about twenty or so in total. Kyle knelt on the far side of the room and took his backpack off, placing it on the floor. As he set the C4 explosive charges, Alex and Jack conducted a secondary sweep of the room.

"All clear." They each had one minute to meet outside the center tent. Just then the earpieces crackled to life.

"Guys, you have to make this quick!" Ben's voice was loud with panic.

Jack slapped his hand over the transmitter to stifle the noise. Kyle and Alex winced and did the same. He took a breath as the men around him galvanized into action, scrambling to get their gear. "Jesus, Ben, do you want them to know we're here with all that yelling?"

Breathing a bit calmer now, Ben replied, "I have at least twenty to thirty heat signatures closing in about a mile out. I can't tell what type of vehicles they have but you can guarantee they're well-armed."

"Shit," Kyle responded. Placing the last charge, he picked up his backpack and said, "Guess someone must have heard the shots."

"How? We didn't see anyone," Alex said.

Walking back toward the entrance, Jack knelt on the ground and moved his hands along the dirt. He saw it before he felt it, a small device with a blinking red light about the size of an old pager. "Fuck," he said, turning to Alex and Kyle. "They have motion detectors now, should have known they would start to think ahead. Let's hurry this up, guys, I don't feel like fighting an army of cartel members. Let's blow this popsicle stand."

"Popsicles do sound good right now," Alex said to himself, as the group exited the tent in a quick succession, lining up on the next tent.

"Nate, can you secure that SUV outside?" Jack asked, now standing in the back of the three-man train.

"Already on it," Nate said.

Jack shouldered his rifle again as team one sat on the other side of the tent waiting to enter. Both teams made entry, but Jack decided not to enter. Hearing a couple of muffled noises, Jack was certain the people who called for backup were hiding inside the center tent.

Once the all-clear came from the radio, Jack ran over to Nate, who managed to find the keys to the vehicle.

"Y'all have to move now, they're half a mile out," Ben said.

"Roger," Jack said. "Nate, get in the driver's seat."

A quick check of his watch showed they had just under two minutes before the complex was going to look like the Fourth of July.

The flap swung open as the quartet sprinted out toward their SUV. Jack swept his rifle across the clearing one last time as he jumped in the back. Nate didn't wait for the last door to close before he stomped on the gas and peeled out in a spray of mud and gravel. Kyle, riding shotgun, reached into his backpack and pulled out two detonators. Handing one to Alex, he lifted the safety and radioed to Ben.

"Hey bud, are we good to blow this joint?" Everyone looked at him with blank faces as if he'd just performed a magic trick. "What? I've always wanted to say that," he said. Just as Nate was going to respond, Ben's voice interrupted.

"Standby, only half the army has entered the compound. I'll let you know when they're all in place."

"Roger." Not twenty seconds later, Ben came back over the radios and said, "Okay, blow it!"

As Alex and Kyle pressed their detonators in the same moment, the reaction was immediate. The ground shook. Nate did his best to keep the SUV on the road from the vibrations. Birds flew in all directions. The team hoped this was the last time they had to come down to this humid hellhole of a place.

"I hope this is truly the last time I ever have to come this far south," Jack said.

CHAPTER 1

Ben Williamson pulled the bright red Nissan Altima into the front of the valet line at the Hilton in downtown San Diego. Opening his door, Ben witnessed the hustle and bustle of the various groups of people laughing and chattering. He handed the valet his ticket, walked behind the car, and grabbed Bri's hand, his Lucchese boots echoing throughout the tile floor.

Bri's Cartier perfume, coupled with her lean five-ten figure, caused men's eyes to divert from their wives and girlfriends to stare at the odd-looking couple as they passed through the lobby. She was only two inches taller than Ben, but her heels, in addition to her elegant poise, often reminded people of a runway model.

Rounding a corner and stopping at the elevator, she said, "I'll be down in ten." Ben felt his face heating up as her wet lipstick touched his puffy cheeks. Smiling and wiping her lipstick off him, she stepped in the elevator and gave him a soft wave. The doors closed. He was a lucky man.

He licked his thumb and rubbed it against his large belt buckle. Adjusting his cowboy hat and looking up, he saw the looks of random shock and awe from various patrons in the lobby. He didn't have to ask why—he already knew. How could a man dressed like he was snag a woman as enthralling as her?

Walking to the hotel bar in the massive lobby and ordering an Old Fashioned, Ben watched the clock hanging on the wall next to him and started a mental countdown in his head while looking at the Lakers basketball game displayed on multiple television screens. They were up 24-8 against the Clippers, the hooting and hollering from the patrons at the bar echoing throughout the lobby. Fifteen minutes went by before he felt skinny fingers run through his short dark hair.

"You ready to go, baby?" Bri asked, who no longer looked like a runway model, but was still beautiful with casual clothes on.

"Fifteen minutes, Bri, I timed you," Ben said, flagging down the bartender.

"Aww, look at my little cowboy. So good with keeping track of the time it takes for me to get ready, but not so good with remembering our two-year anniversary," she said, smiling. Ben ignored the last comment and signed the check.

"Bri, I brought you to San Diego, isn't that enough?" He asked. They left the hotel, headed toward Moonshine Flats, one of two country bars within walking distance.

"Baby, you're so cute," Bri said, wrapping her hands in his and kissing him on the cheek again. Her nice blue jeans, low-cut top exposing the tops of her breasts, and heels still displayed a level of beauty about her that caused Ben to smile. It didn't really matter what she wore.

Pablo, Santiago, and Matias sat in their SUV one block up from the country bar. Working as a sicario in the Saint Bertrand Cartel had its perks, and these three were some of the deadliest combinations of the many sicarios Alejandro Alvarez had working for him.

Alejandro was exhausted listening to constant reports of his narco-submarines and various cocaine-processing compounds constantly being burned to the ground in the middle of the rainforest. Smuggling cocaine was a billion-dollar enterprise and he was not going to see his go to waste. The cartel had an infinite supply of funds, and Alejandro exhausted every resource to find who was at the helm of the ship destroying his property. Once he discovered it was a special operations team from the United States using a small abandoned army base in the middle of the rainforest, he knew what had to come next.

He contacted his lawyer, who in turn contacted a friend who was well oriented in the dark web. Through some backdoor negotiating, he was able to acquire the name of a CIA analyst who specialized in giving out secret information for the right price. Pablo, as per Alejandro's orders, contacted her and offered a hefty paycheck in return for just a name of one of the operators involved. Once she agreed to the terms, the money was wired and Ben Williamson's name was supplied.

"*Maricón*, these tacos are shit compared to the ones back home," Santiago said, stuffing his face with the third taco.

"Yeah? Then stop stuffing your face with them and maybe I'll believe you, *ese*," Matias said from the backseat, who just got back from a food truck close by.

"Where are these *wedo's*?" Pablo asked, reaching back to Matias and motioning for him to give him another soft-shelled taco. Setting it on his lap below the steering wheel, he opened the aluminum foil and poured some of the hot sauce over it.

"They had better show up at this stupid bar," Matias said, turning his wrist to look at his watch. Nine o'clock.

"*Mira*, they're coming, okay? *Cálmate*, I heard them in the clothing store earlier today. *Estarán aquí*," Santiago said, grunting as he stuffed his face with another taco. Looking at the different crowds walk past their dark SUV, he spotted their targets.

"There they are," Pablo said, nudging his head toward the entrance and swallowing a mouthful of steak.

Ben grabbed their two cocktails and made his way through the crowd to the back of the bar where Bri was located. Setting their drinks on the table, Ben peeked at his girlfriend.

"Can you please stop checking your Insta-feed?" Glaring back at him, she responded, "Baby, I'm checking my email from my professor about what's required for class this semester. But don't worry, this is graduate school stuff, I wouldn't expect you to understand," she said with a devilish grin.

Dropping his jaw, he said, "How do you always have a smart-ass answer? I'm supposed to be that person."

She put her phone in her pocket and moved closer to Ben, wrapping her arms around his neck. Her green eyes stared down into his hazel ones as if she were looking into his soul. "Okay, baby, you can be the smart-ass and I'll just take it." She winked at him and kissed his lips, sending waves of euphoria throughout his body.

She pulled away and allowed Ben to grab his drink and take a sip. "This place is pretty slammed for a Wednesday," he said.

"Summer is also almost over, so all of us college students have to get our last hurrahs in before school starts up."

"Damn, that's right," Ben said, taking a bigger sip of his Old Fashioned. Bri was in graduate school to become a lawyer, and he knew that she was way smarter than he could ever be. Besides, with a job like his, why bother going back to school? He had his undergrad degree with a decent-paying job as a tech guru for an off-the-books CIA gig. Life was good.

The night went on, and when both of their drinks were finished, Ben grabbed them and headed back to order another round. He bobbed and weaved his way to the counter, leaned over, and raised his arm to the stunning redheaded bartender with loads of tattoos. Walking over in her daisy dukes, bright red lipstick, and pigtails, she gave Ben a smile.

"Same two cocktails, hun?" she asked—clearly a local with no country accent, but just playing the part.

"You have a pretty good memory with all these other people in here."

"Yeah, well, I always remember the handsome ones," she said, smiling and winking. She turned around to get the next round of drinks. Ben couldn't help but watch her walk away and at that exact moment as he felt a heavy hand land on his shoulder.

"Amigo!" The Hispanic gentleman in the white Lacoste button-up reeked of cigarettes. The other man who was with him was dressed very similar and walked around to stand on Ben's other side.

"Can I help you?" Ben asked, leaning into the man, barely able to understand his heavy accent. He looked down and saw their Lampasas cowboy boots. Whoever they were had great taste.

"We were about to take these tequila shots, my friend, but our other buddy is taking a piss. We also don't feel like waiting for him, so we saw you by yourself over here and was wondering if you wanted to take one with us really quick?"

Looking back at his fiancé through the crowd—still on her phone, he noticed—he couldn't resist. "Why not," he said, "I can never turn down a shot!" After serving Ben his two cocktails, the waitress retrieved a bottle of 1800 Tequila from the top shelf and poured three glasses. The man with his hand on Ben's shoulder introduced himself as Santiago, and Matias did the same. All three men slammed the shots in quick succession as Ben thanked him. He hurried back to Bri with his drinks in hand. After midnight, the crowd started to die down. Bri yawned a couple of times, Ben kissed her, telling her they would walk back after he returned from the restroom.

Pablo had moved the SUV, parked it off to one side in the alley behind the bar, and stepped out with his suppressed Glock 19 in the small of his back. Dumping his Cohiba cigar embers on the ground, he felt his phone vibrating in his pocket. "About time," he said, pressing his finger against the fingerprint scanner to unlock the phone. Reading the text message, he nodded, and shoved the phone back into his pocket. Stomping out the cigar, he looked down the long alleyway. The only witnesses he could think of, or see for that matter, were the ones passing by occasionally on the sidewalk forty or so yards in front of their SUV. Getting back into the driver's seat, he cranked the engine.

There was a long hallway in the back of the club that separated the kitchen on the right from the restrooms on the left. The men's restroom was in the back closest to the emergency exit ending the pathway down the hall. Even though the sign on the door said "alarm will sound," the sicarios watched as they constantly saw patrons leave through the door all night. Leaving the restroom, Ben didn't make it five feet before running into Santiago and Matias.

"Hey!" Ben said, throwing his arms into the sky like a referee signaling a touchdown. The two sicarios looked at each other and checked behind them. Sure, people were around, but nobody was paying any attention. "You guys, let me buy you a each a shot this time."

"Sure," Santiago said. "You said you were from Texas, right?"

"Originally, yeah, but I live in Virginia now, why?"

"I'm thinking about moving to Texas, but I can't decide where. It's too expensive to live out here," Santiago said. These Americans were so gullible when they got drinks in their system.

"Oh, perfect, where are you trying to live?" Ben asked, very inquisitive now that this stranger was talking about his home state.

"Let's take a step outside," Santiago said, "I'm going to smoke, and we can chat while I do. It's a little stuffy in here."

Ben looked back in the direction of Bri and shrugged. Santiago led the way and Matias followed up behind Ben. Stepping outside, and walking just out of eyesight from the door, he lit his cigarette and spoke. It was at this moment Matias noticed they were alone in the alleyway. He reached into his blazer pocket and pulled out a syringe. He stabbed Ben in the neck and pushed the orange rod down, watching the sleep serum flow through the clear syringe. Matias caught Ben just as his knees buckled. Pablo pulled up next to them and jumped out to open the back door and help shove the body inside.

"Took you idiots long enough!" he snapped.

"Shut it, *pendejo*," Santiago said, taking one long drag from his cigarette and flicking it off to the side. Doing one last look around, all three sicarios hopped into the SUV and sped off into the night.

CHAPTER 2

Jack Knowles hadn't even finished turning onto the stone-covered sidewalk before seeing the familiar blacked-out federal SUV pull up behind him. Still walking, knowing exactly who would waste time trying to find him instead of making a simple phone call, he sighed.

"Jack, next time you decide to not brief me and go above my head to ask for authorization for a mission, I'll have your head on a platter," Janet Carrera said.

"Hey, we needed our first real mission and I saw an opportunity to take it. You weren't around to ask," Jack replied sarcastically.

"You could have called and left a message. David chewed me out for twenty minutes."

"Sorry," Jack said.

"You're not sorry!" Janet snapped. "You have any idea how that made me look? Let me remind you of my job because clearly you forgot. I divvy out all of the assignments to the agents, who to kill, what information we need, and most importantly, who gets what assignments. I've been around the block a few times, Jack. I know what I'm doing."

"You think being a field analyst studying terrorists for most of your career gives you permission to be the biggest and craziest on the block? You were given this job because you happened to help Max and I find Khaled Ahmadi in a warehouse three years ago. You know, I would have thought the Director of Clandestine Operations would be more cautious than trying to do a meet and greet in broad daylight," Jack said, sipping his vanilla latte.

"What's even more suspicious is a person talking to a blacked-out SUV following him on the sidewalk. Get in," she said.

Jack looked to his right as a group of college schoolgirls laughed. "And here I was thinking that this little cafe was enough off the books for no one to know about it." He opened the door and slid in. Her perfume was the first thing he could smell as the SUV pulled away from the curb. It reminded him of his late wife, and he had to admit to himself, she had good taste.

"We're the CIA, Jack. We know where our members are at all times," she said, raising her penciled-in eyebrows. She was very attractive at forty-two, and her clothes fit so tightly explained to anyone who spent just five seconds looking at her that she was a glutton for punishment in the gym.

"What do you want? I have a boating trip with some friends you're delaying my departure for."

She adjusted her posture and brushed her shoulder-length dirty-blonde hair off her face. "I didn't know you had any friends," she said, throwing her hands in the air in a surrender pose.

Jack took a sip from his latte as his patience was wearing thin. Struggling to hold his tongue, he said, "What do you want? It's Friday morning."

"Which means it's still part of the work day, right?" she said, rolling her eyes. "Anyway, I hate to be the bearer of bad news but your fishing trip is going to have to be put on hold." She reached inside the pocket of the seat in front of her and pulled out a manila folder.

"What's this?" he said, setting his latte in the cup holder, picking at the tape that wrapped the top of the envelope. She quickly put a hand on top of his, stopping him abruptly.

"This just got awkward," he said, giving her a blank stare. "I at least want to be wined and dined first."

"This is serious," she said, quickly removing her hand.

"Okay, well, why don't you front-load me then?" he said, sitting up straighter in his seat now.

"I don't have time to brief you right now because if I sit here while you open that you'll have a million and one questions. Also, I have to be back at work to deal with the contents of that envelope," she said. Jack took a deep breath, tucked the envelope in the small of his back, and grabbed his latte from out of the holder.

"You know—"

"Excuse me," Interrupted Jack, opening the door and stepping outside. If Janet was a cartoon, smoke would have been billowing from her ears. "I hope you have a good weekend." Jack just stood there with the door open, admiring the words that just left his lips. Was he out of line? Absolutely. But he had been waiting to throw her off her cloud for a long time and this was the opportunity that presented itself.

"Close my door," she said, as he kicked it shut. "And by the way, you missed a middle button," she replied, looking at his shirt and flipping him the bird.

He laughed but did not give her the satisfaction looking at his shirt until the SUV was out of sight. "I actually did miss a button. What a way to start the weekend."

CHAPTER 3

Jack had everyone meet at what the team called "the Office," which was in reality a four-thousand square foot mansion sitting in a gated community behind a golf course. When Jack was asked by his best friend, David Carter, to spearhead the new off-the-books clandestine group for the agency, he only had one request: ensure that his Bering Group did not have to go through the rigorous checkpoints of reporting to the agency every day. Through some negotiating that David was able to secure with the finance department—being the Director of the agency had its perks—Jack was given a month to find a place to lease. He only needed a week.

The estate was all well-surrounded with trees and shrubbery, and on the outskirts of it all was a luscious golf course that ranked in the top twenty on the Eastern sea border. The old, Victorian-style mansion, which happened to sit on two acres of land, was purchased in Gainesville, just thirty-eight minutes from the CIA headquarters in Langley, Virginia. Over the course of the next two months, which gave Jack plenty of time to recruit his members, it was transformed and renovated into a glorified safe house for the team that was hidden in plain sight. The neighborhood, Green Falls Manor, had security guards at the front gate, who were later replaced by newly recruited agency operatives from the CIA who paid the security group enough money to say "we'll take it from here." This made it possible to add an extra layer of security so the Bering Group always knew who was coming in and out of the complex.

"Okay," Jack said, "sorry to spoil your weekends, but Janet wanted me to open this envelope today." The tape ripping from the manila folder was the only sound. The six members— Kyle, Courtney, Pete, Kwame, Alex, and Nate—were all sitting in the theater room which was outfitted with soundproof walls. Jack stood in front of the computer screen and held a small white USB flash drive from the envelope. Jack flipped his wrist over, scanning his Omega Aqua Terra, which read just after ten o'clock. Part of the Omega *worldtimer* collection, this was by far the prettiest watch he ever owned. "So much for that fishing trip," he mumbled to himself, trying to find the right files to pull up on the computer.

"This better be good, my boyfriend booked a couple's massage today that I had to pass on," Courtney said, not happy to be at work on a Friday. Pulling her ponytail from dangling behind her chair, she intertwined it within her fingers. Courtney Dixon was the shortest at five foot five, but she could handle herself just like if not better than any of the guys she worked with. Born and raised in Anchorage, Alaska along with her four brothers and one sister, she was more than comfortable being called, 'one of the guys'. She was young and the only woman in the group, but at twenty nine years old she had more than enough credentials to roll around with the toughest men. After high school she applied for the Anchorage Police Department and after growing up in the city, and knowing the police chief personally, she was an easy pick. Not having much to do in Anchorage, she was an avid fisher, hunter, and a black belt in Brazilian Ju Jitsu.

Excelling quickly throughout the department with constant drug busts, criminal apprehensions and minor infractions, she was known as a no-nonsense kind of woman and quickly earned the respect of the men around her. She even joined the Special Weapons and Tactics team, the first female to do so in the city. Courtney was on top of the world and found her calling, or at least thought she did. After eleven years of the same dog and pony show, dealing with the same criminals and often raiding the same houses she wanted a new challenge. All of her other siblings took the opportunity to move from Alaska the first chance they had and were always trying to get her to do something more, often telling her she had a higher calling. As it turned out, eleven years was the tipping point as she looked for more careers in the government, the CIA came to mind. Not knowing anyone in that line of work she figured that would be the next best challenge. After applying and waiting several months for a response, she was selected.

"Perks of the job, Miss Courtney," Jack said.

Kwame, the six-foot-five ex-Nigerian special forces, said, "Didn't you say a couple days ago that you caught him talking to one of his exes on Instagram or something?"

"Yeah," she sighed. "We talked for a while and he said he was sorry, but I still have this feeling in my gut like he's lying or something, I don't know." Her deep Southern drawl only decided to leave her lips when she was annoyed or stressed, and she was both.

"Oh, fuck him," Kyle said, smirking and looking at Pete, usually his partner in crime. But Pete was shaking his head and continued to look at his phone. Kyle Wright and Pete McKinley were always together despite the fact their personalities couldn't be further apart. Pete was the nice one from Tampa, Florida and Kyle was the 'hard-headed' one from the south side of Boston, yet somehow they seemed to click. Courtney however, hated when Kyle's Boston way of thinking got the better of him, although she never pulled her punches.

"I don't remember anyone talking to you. Are all you North-Easterner's idiots or is that just you?" Courtney replied, turning around to address Kyle, who was from Boston.

"Well," Kyle said, reclining his seat, "you can't be the love of his life if he's off talking to other broads. Plus, it's a day spa and I don't know any guy who likes those."

Her blood boiled. "Have you ever thought that maybe, just maybe, there is a reason why you're single?"

"You two are like children," Kwame said. "If she loves someone then let her love. You Americans are so different than us," he said, laughing to himself as he too reclined his seat.

"Oh really, and how would you handle this situation?" Kyle asked, teasing him.

Kwame leaned over into Kyle's ear and said with a feint whisper, "Listen here, you wouldn't last a day with African women. They would chew you up and spit you back out." Kyle flipped him the bird as Pete let out a laugh.

"Now, that was funny!" he said, sliding his phone in his pocket.

Jack stood back from the computer and raised his hand as everyone quieted down to give him undivided attention.

"Okay, let's get this over with," Jack said, signaling to Kwame to get the lights in the back of the room.

The recliner moaned in agony as Kwame's powerlifter frame build stood up to walk over to shut the lights off. The only glow in the room now was the light emulating from the screen.

On the projection screen was a thirty-second video clip of what appeared to be some alleyway behind what they could only guess was a nightclub. The footage wasn't very clear but they could see three men walking outside. A couple of seconds passed as one of the men pulled out a cigarette and lit it as the third man in the back pulled something out of his pocket and stuck the man in the middle in the neck. As the man fell, an SUV pulled up and a fourth person hopped out to help load the body into the back. Within a matter of seconds all individuals were inside the SUV as it sped away.

The video stopped and froze at the empty alleyway for five more seconds before it went dark. Pete was first to speak up, "Rewind the footage if you don't mind."

"Not at all."

The screen turned back on as all the events played backward in a slow succession. "Stop!" Pete yelled.

The image now frozen were three individuals right before the middle man was stabbed in the neck.

"Who are we looking at?" Courtney asked, who was now squinting at the man getting stabbed in the neck.

"I guess that's the million-dollar question," Jack replied, walking up to the screen.

"Can you zoom in at all?" Alex asked. He was the only Hispanic speaker on the team and being raised in Dallas, Texas his southern drawl in conjunction with a light Puerto Rican accent came out when he got excited. Although he was not as big as Kwame, he was next in line for most muscular member of the group. Standing at five foot eleven with brown eyes and dark brown hair, he resembled a model one would see on the cover of any fitness magazine.

"Yeah, standby," Jack said, walking back over to the keyboard.

"The timestamp on the bottom right corner says Wednesday morning," Nate said, who was just as confused as everyone else in the room. "So, at 12:06 on Wednesday, three people were standing outside this...what I guess is a club...and one person was kidnapped?"

Jack leaned into the computer screen instead of the projector. "The video is too fuzzy to make out anything," he said.

"Hey Jack, didn't you say Janet wanted you to call her after we watched all this?" Alex asked, who was now standing right next to the edge of the screen trying to look as closely as possible to make out any details in the picture.

"Ah shit, that's right," Jack exclaimed, reaching into his pocket to pull out his phone. The room fell silent as a couple more people stood up and walked over to the massive screen to try and make out any other details. Not thirty seconds went by before Jack was already screaming at Janet through the phone.

"You're serious, and you're just now telling me this?" After Jack stepped out of the room to finish his conversation in private, everyone went back to trying to decipher the video. Five minutes went by before Jack stepped back into the room, shutting the door behind him.

"What's up? What did she say?" Pete said, once again breaking the silence.

Shaking his head in confusion, Jack said, "Apparently, the tech division ran the facial recognition data through the software and those are Alejandro Alvarez's sicarios and Ben."

The room went silent and nobody said a word for a good minute. Reality was sinking in fast.

"Why are we just now seeing this? The time stamp said Wednesday morning, it's Friday almost noon," Kwame said, his massive forearms crossed.

"That's a good question."

CHAPTER 4

"Janet, why am I just hearing about this two days later?" Jack had left the mansion like a bat out of hell, drove to the agency and stormed into David's office to see Janet sitting in it already. David was sitting behind his gigantic mahogany desk on the infamous seventh floor, which was reserved for the director of the agency and everyone who worked directly for him.

"You weren't around, and the analysts had to be sure it was Ben kidnapped in the video," Janet said with a smug expression. "Janet," he began, but stopped when he heard the door opening up as David's secretary peered inside, "Is everything alright?"

"It's fine, thanks," David responded, waving his hand up, instructing her to close the door. Closing his eyes, he removed his glasses sliding down his clean-shaven face and massaged the sides of his temples. David said, "You two are going to cause me to have a heart attack."

"You both know there's a pecking order here, and keeping me out of the loop doesn't cut it. I have nothing but the best interest in your team, Jack," she stated, crossing her legs.

"And that's your justification for keeping us in the dark for a couple of days? How does that fit into all of this?" Jack responded, one more comment away from telling Janet to screw off.

"You act like it was a week! I mean, come on, the footage showed he was kidnapped early Wednesday morning and I met you literally less than forty-eight hours later. Cut me some slack," she said.

"Riddle me this, Batman, how and when exactly did you find out he was kidnapped?" Jack asked, standing behind the chair next to

Janet. His anger was getting the better of him before he even showed up—he almost blew through two red light cameras just to get here.

David held up his hand once more and leaned back in his squeaky leather chair. "Janet, do you mind giving us a minute?"

Looking at them both, she nodded and stood. She reached out and adjusted David's coffee cup so it lined up perfectly with the coaster. Jack scoffed. She shot him one last dirty look.

"If you need me, I'll be in my office," she said, pushing in her chair so it lined up with the front edge of David's desk. The room fell silent. As she shut the door behind her, David pulled out a bottle of Eagle Rare from a drawer along with two glasses.

"You know, you never get used to her awkwardness," David said.

Jack shook his head and watched his friend pour them each a drink, not even fathoming what was going through Ben's head at the moment. Jack had so many questions of his own—mainly, why Ben? Ben wasn't even one of the operators on the ground, he was flying at forty-thousand feet in the air. David slid a glass across the desk and took a sip from his own. "You know I've known you for over thirty years now and I have never seen you get so pissed that you might strangle someone."

Jack humored him with a small chuckle and took a sip. Standing up and walking over to the bookcase to his left, Jack surveyed the collection of novels that never ceased to amaze him.

"You're not smart enough to read, David," Jack said, grabbing one of the thicker books on philosophy. David laughed. Flipping through the pages and placing it back on the shelf, Jack walked over to the massive window that ran behind David's desk. The view was incredible and being the Director did have its perks.

"Most of those books were gifts, believe it or not. However, what I *can* read is the information that your lover over there pulled up for you guys." Opening a drawer to his left, he pulled out a red file and tossed it over to Jack, who took his seat once more.

David leaned back in his chair as he watched Jack skim through the information.

"Lover! God help any man who would want to get with that woman."

Staying silent but swiveling his chair behind him to look out at the beautiful view of the compound with the trees in the distance that seemed to touch the horizon, David said, "Anyway, they were also able to run the plates of the SUV, which came back registered to a Mr. James Clark, reported stolen early that morning."

"Of course it was, and I take it they ran his name?"

"Yep, it looks like he's a white male who lives in Temecula, a county outside of San Diego. Mr. Clark, who has no priors, owns a tech business and has a wife and two kids. He checks out," answered David, sipping on his bourbon.

"Do we know the names of the individuals yet? When I talked to her earlier, she didn't have them," Jack said, looking at the faces of the cartel members.

"Yes, since then the software recognized the faces and came back with three individuals, all part of Alejandro's Bertrand Cartel."

"Fuck," Jack said, finishing his bourbon.

"Matias Sanchez, Santiago Juarez, and Pablo Estevez of your Saint Bertrand Cartel. You want to know the best part?"

"What's that?"

"They're not just some random soldiers in his cartel, they're sicarios. The camera didn't pick it up, but if you look at the mug shots we have on file courtesy of the Colombian Embassy, they all have the famous small saint tattoo behind their left ear."

"Damn," Jack said, holding one of the images in front of him, finally looking up from the file. "So they know what they're doing. How did we even get this footage?"

"They kidnapped him early Thursday morning and after his girlfriend filed a missing person report with the police later that morning, she called Ben's parents. When she was done with them, she posted something on social media around 10 a.m. our time and our department pulled in up within minutes. We would have found out regardless once the police put their report into the system, but her posting it definitely started the ball rolling.

"She'll be alright though, she's with her family back in Tennessee right now. Believe me, I wanted to call you, but Janet's right on this one. I know you were against her getting promoted a year ago, but she has been nothing but extremely helpful to me in creating your task force and keeping it off the books. You realize the President of the United States doesn't even know about you guys, right? The fucking *President*."

"Yeah, yeah, I know," Jack said, pouring some more bourbon into his glass.

David watched Jack lean back in his seat once more. They both had been through a lot. Entering the agency together and passing the FARM with flying colors, they were roommates and clicked since day one. Jack had been the best man at David's wedding; he was like family. Jack even had his own key to David's house to check on his family when he had to go away for business. There was no one he thought would be better suited to lead the off-the-books task force. Jack named the group based off his secret missions he conducted in Alaska for multiple months helping other agents spy on the Russians. It was there where he realized the Bering Sea was unforgiving in the winter, but in the summer was as smooth as glass—so what better name for a team that was cool, calm, and collected until they had to get their hands dirty?

"So what do you want us to do, man?" Jack responded, sliding the file back toward David, who immediately returned it.

"We have plenty of copies. You now have a copy of the SUV plates in the file as well. We have him tracked to a town in Nogales, Arizona." David poured himself another glass.

"Why are they driving all the way to Arizona?"

"It's what our intelligence has gathered from tracking the plates via satellite. Also, if you care for a little light reading later, Alejandro isn't on the best of terms with the cartel working out of Baja, Mexico. Pushing further east and then heading down might work out better for him."

"Interesting."

David held his hand up to let him finish. "The club they were outside of is one of only two cowboy clubs in downtown San Diego. The local police report said the bartender vaguely remembers Ben, but she does remember two men whose hands and necks were covered with tattoos. Anyway, Nogales is near the border and has a history for harboring illegal aliens and other various criminal activity. Janet suggested we send the whole squad down there to figure it out, but I ruled against it."

"That's why she has no business in this business—"

"Enough. I get it you hate her. Now let me finish," David said. "We have satellite imagery monitoring the house they stopped at. This will be your second assignment with the group and I'm sorry for the circumstances of it. I know I don't have to micromanage you or your team, but Janet will be taking point on this. You have to give her the time of day Jack, she is your boss for Christ's sake. Plus, I have a shit-storm of my own to deal with regarding all of this, but don't get confused: if you need anything at all, you let me know." David reached across the table to shake his friend's hand.

After letting the last comment linger in the air for a bit as Jack sipped on his scotch once more, David asked, "Do you have a plan of attack for this?"

"Yea, I do," he replied, stroking his grayish stubble. Jack was about to stand up, but David quickly motioned for him to sit back down.

"What is it?"

"One last thing."

Jack could tell by his body language that whatever his best friend was about to say was weighing heavy on his mind. Spinning his chair around once more to the window, David said, "I want to bring him back from the field to integrate him with your team."

"Bring who back?" Jack said.

"Fontaine."

The room fell silent. The faint chattering of birds could be heard flying just outside the massive windows. Stroking his chin again, Jack thought carefully about the next words leaving his lips. "Are you sure you want the old squad back in business?" Both men laughed.

"You and I both know that neither one of us needs to be running and gunning out there on wild goose chases looking for bad guys in today's world. Back when we were coming up, times were different, and to be frank I didn't bring you in on this project so you could go out there with your team.

"You're the best in the business as far as I'm concerned, your experience coupled with your longevity with the agency far surpasses anyone else. You and I both know you've seen more than anyone here and shoot, you've definitely accomplished a hell of a lot more in a shorter time span than most of these new operators we have in the field now."

Jack couldn't believe what he was hearing. On the one hand he greatly appreciated everything his friend was revealing to him, and he knew every word he was hearing was one hundred percent true, however on the other hand, one of the stipulations to the group was getting to select whom he wanted on the team.

"I love that kid, I just never thought we would get approval to be back together again."

"I know, but look who your boss is," he said, excitedly. "I literally can authorize anything I want or need."

"Your mind is made up then, you want him with us? You said I get to hand select my team. I don't want you calling me a month from now asking if we can draft some more people. This isn't NFL draft day."

"I get it," David said. His face told Jack all he needed to know about his time being up in his office.

Downing the last bit of bourbon, Jack stood up a second time and didn't receive the wave to sit back down. "I'll give him a shout as soon as I leave, and see if I can't twist his arm to get him to fly in."

"No, I want you to fly down and recruit him in person."

"Fly down? Where is he?" he asked.

Laughing, David said, "He's in West Palm Beach."

"Florida?! Great God almighty, I have never had assignments in Florida, especially this time of year. What the hell kind of work do you guys have him doing down there?" Jack asked, as most if not all of the work assigned to anyone was overseas and rarely ever domestic.

"He's on vacay," David replied.

"Of course." Turning to leave his office, Jack thanked his friend for the drink. Reminiscing of the times with Max, the last thing he remembered was that they both got into a serious predicament when a little girl was killed inside of a country where they were not supposed to be. They were tasked with monitoring Khaled Ahmadi, a very dangerous terrorist who was selling a stolen list of every undercover agent for the CIA. Jack and Max were given a capture or kill order for Khaled before things went south.

Once Jack was back in his vehicle, he dialed Pete and told him who he wanted on a flight to Nogales. Deep down he knew David was right to recruit Max; he was very seldom wrong. But he never thought he was ever going to have the chance to work with his old partner. He would have to make sure this time around, everything was done right.

CHAPTER 5

Saint Bertrand, better known as Saint Louis Bertrand to those who worshipped him, was the first Saint to arrive in Colombia in the sixteenth century. Some said it was because of him that Colombia had such a gigantic Catholic culture, and although many saints visited Colombia, he was the absolute first, making him the go-to saint to be worshipped by Columbians.

The most important person to dedicate his life to the Catholic Saint of Saints was Alejandro Alvarez. Growing up in Cartagena, Colombia was a gift as far as he was concerned. Raised by his uncle because both his parents died in a car accident when he was only twelve, he was forced to grow up sooner than the children around him. His uncle, Juan Alvarez, was the leader of the Bertrand Cartel, which made him one of the most feared and revered men in all of Cartagena. Even the other cartels in the neighboring countries did not want to deal with Juan because of what they heard he did to people who did not deliver the promises requested on time.

Money and resources were never an issue for Alejandro because of his uncle. Juan wanted him to achieve what his parents would have wanted: a college education. Alejandro graduated high school in the top ten of his class and wanted to continue his college in Colombia, yet Juan persuaded him to apply for more challenging ones in North America. The acceptance letters arrived in droves, but the one that gained his attention—well, the beautiful women in the area, did—was Berkeley University where he graduated with an undergraduate degree in Business Administration. Catching the first plane back to his hometown after graduation, the only thing he wanted to do was help his uncle with new and more updated business ideas. Unfortunately, within the first year of returning home, Juan was diagnosed with stage four stomach cancer and died soon after. Being the last in the bloodline of the Alvarez family, who better to take his spot than Alejandro himself.

Sitting on his veranda overlooking the gorgeous countryside at his massive estate that he now inherited, he received a phone call from one of his sicarios. Putting the newspaper down on the glass table, he took one more sip of coffee and answered the call.

"*Buenos Días*, Pablo, *cómo estás?*"

"*Bien, jefe*. We might have a bit of a problem."

Sighing, he said, "Well, what is it?"

"You remember our informant, *la rubia*?"

"Sí, I'm imagining you have some information for me otherwise you wouldn't be making this call, am I correct?" Alejandro asked, who wanted more than anything to just get back to enjoying the sun's rays.

"She said they have a team leaving to our location as we speak."

With this new information, Alejandro stood up, stretched, and leaned over his balcony, eying one of his lovely girlfriends who was sunbathing by the pool below. The cartel drug lord took another sip of his coffee and responded, "How far are they out?"

"She didn't say, *jefe*, just that there was going to be a team leaving to our location. My only question is, how did they find out where we are?"

Rubbing his eyes at the ignorance, he said, "The technique is quite simple. Law enforcement agencies track vehicles all the time. They use their traffic cameras to jump from one camera to the next when the license plate they're looking for crosses in front of another camera. This allows them to accurately locate any vehicle in they need so long as it passes by one of the cameras. I told you idiots to get rid of the stolen car, *pendejo*!"

"Sorry, *jefe*. So what do you want to do?"

There was a long pause before Alejandro continued speaking.

"Stick with the original plan, and no more fuck-ups," Alejandro said and ended the call. Shutting his eyes and running his fingers through his slicked-back hair, he squeezed the phone so hard he was certain it would snap. But then he relaxed. Panic attacks ran in his family, and he had learned over the years, with a few expensive therapy sessions, that a couple of deep breaths usually did the trick.

CHAPTER 6

The three Old Fashioned's kept Jack occupied on the Gulfstream G550 into Opa Locka Executive Airport in Florida, allowing a small buzz to creep into his system. Looking at his watch, he knew the team would be landing in Phoenix within the next couple of hours. Upon landing, a small sedan was waiting for him inside of the hangar. After getting situated in the car, he reached underneath the passenger seat and stopped when he felt a small plastic case. Keeping him company on the drive North was a Glock 19 with an Omega 9k silencer. He could never be too careful in this business.

Cruising up the One, Jack overlooked some of the clearest water he had ever had the pleasure of swimming in. He reminisced on simpler times with his wife who had lost her battle with breast cancer five years prior, and wished that this was a vacation pit-stop instead of business. Thinking of ways to convince his former partner to work with him again wouldn't be too hard—at least he thought. Reaching over to the volume knob and twisting it to the left, the sounds of Yanni disappeared from his ears. The only sound now was the rumbling of the tires over the highway. Dialing Max's phone for the third time, he was hopeful Max would answer, but it went to voicemail, again. He found the courage to leave a voicemail, giving Max a time and place to meet.

After checking in and cleaning up, Jack headed downstairs, out the front door, and straight over to the bars and restaurants that lined the strip where his hotel was sitting. This would be a very short trip so coming up with a plan of attack as to how he would pitch the idea was of the utmost importance.

Jack walked into one of the bars ignited with tiki torches giving off an island feel. Deciding to take a seat with a view admiring
the ocean instead of the television at the bar, he took a deep breath
and basked at the beautiful horizon as the last of the sun's rays
beat down on the ocean.

Finishing his meal and not seeing Max yet, he decided to order
a drink. Five minutes later, as the waitress walked over to his table
to bring his Mojito, his work phone rang. Waiting for the waitress
to walk away first, he answered the call. It was Pete.

"What do you have?" Jack asked, leaning back in his chair.

"I take it Janet didn't update you?"

"What do you mean?"

"We tracked the vehicle to a house in Nogales, no dice. The
SUV was still in the driveway when we cleared the house too."

"Jesus," Jack said.

"Sweeping the house, we found a tunnel in the pantry, and I
know I don't need to tell you where I think it probably leads. We
also found fresh cigarette ashes on the counter, so we figured we
were right behind them."

"I'm glad you didn't venture down into the tunnel. No telling
what kind of traps you guys just avoided."

"Agreed," Pete said. There was a long pause and Jack knew
there was something Pete wasn't telling him.

"What is it?"

"The last thing we found was a note on the counter next to the
ashes. It said, 'come and get us, gringos'."

"Dammit," Jack said, rubbing his eyes. "Did you tell anyone
about the note?"

"No, you're the first."

"Good, let's keep it that way. If they knew we were coming, then someone on our end is feeding them information.
We'll have to play this one close to the chest until I can get any

further info. Until then, head back to Virginia and I'll see you in the morning."

"I expect you to have a little bit of fun while you're down there," Pete said. "Those women in Florida are on another level of gorgeous."

Sighing, Jack responded, "Goodbye, Pete."

Just then, a familiar voice said from behind him, "A mole, huh? What are you trying to get me into? You're getting too old for this, you know." The dark-skinned athletic-framed individual walked past Jack, tossing a polaroid on the table. Grabbing the seat across from his old partner, Max picked up the menu and looked it over.

"Jesus, Max, a Polaroid? At least treat me with some dignity and respect." Jack took out his cell phone and pulled up an image of his own. Jack's image was of his rear-view mirror and depicted Max sitting two car lengths behind him at a traffic light in Fort Lauderdale. Reaching over and grabbing the polaroid, Jack said, "You didn't even catch my good side."

"Is that your excuse when anyone takes an unsolicited picture of you grabbing your luggage at the airport?" Max laughed.

Jack signaled the waitress to come over to the table and watched his old partner bombard her with a volley of questions, half flirting and half about the cocktail menu.

Jack hadn't seen his friend in over six years and he looked good for being deployed all the time. Max's lumberjack beard showed hints of grey not too unlike Jack's own, and was a friendly reminder that both operators were aging. Once the waitress walked away with his order, Jack saw the beady brown eyes staring back at him and could tell by the inquisitive look on his face Max wanted to get right to business.

"Well, old friend, how are you?" Jack said, leaning back in his chair.

"Not too bad, man, just on vacation here as I'm sure you can tell."

"Damn," Jack said with a slick response in between sips of his beer. "Whatever they have you doing at the agency must be nice if you have time for vacation."

Max laughed. "Yeah, as I'm sure you're aware now, I work alone."

"David might have mentioned it," Jack replied.

The closest people sitting next to them were ten paces away at the bar. Leaning in close, Jack's seriousness began. "So what have you been doing all these years after the Khaled op?"

"Nothing, just riding solo. David convinced the DNI that I would be less of an asset to the agency if they were to put me behind a desk," Max said.

The only person David Carter reported to was the Director of National Intelligence, Alexis Moore. She would be the one briefing the president of any and all CIA matters during their National Security Council briefs. She was also the main reason and the absolute last line of security from the president finding out about the Bering Group. Somebody needed to operate with impunity to handle terrorism, no matter what kind reared its ugly head and an off the books task force was the way to do it. Killing, torture, you name it it was green-lit. After all, what the president didn't know, wouldn't hurt him.

Giving him a blank stare, Jack said, "I wish they thought that way about me at the time."

"You're also older than I am Jack, but I can't blame you for getting mad when they made you an instructor. Honestly, I can see why David did it. All you did was slow me down." Max took a swig from his drink. Jack chuckled and took another sip from his beer.

Sitting in his chair, looking out into the vast ocean, Jack thought for a second or two before he said, "I take it you already know about my group then?"

"I knew about you after David told me that he was picking you to lead the team. You realize I was the first person he asked to join, right?"

"Somehow I'm not surprised," Jack whispered under his breath. "I take it you've heard about our current situation?"

Finishing his drink, Max replied, "I don't know anything past the initial kidnapping. I was told you were going to brief me on any current events."

"Not here. There's a seat, more like an empty first class cabin, with your name on it. We leave tomorrow afternoon."

"Hold on a minute," Max said. holding up his hand. "I like my current job. I love working with you and have nothing but respect for you, but if I agree to help you it's strictly a favor to you. Nothing more. I'll work with this crew of misfit toys you've assembled, but for the record, you're the only person I've ever worked with, and quite frankly I work best alone."

Laughing, Jack said, "Fair enough."

"Tell me about the rest of the hooligans you've assembled."

"There's a smartass, a couple of chill people, an attractive blonde, a guy who can pretty much bench you and me at the same time, and then there's me." Jack gave a courteous bow at the table.

Shaking his head and smiling, Max responded, "That doesn't give me any information whatsoever, but I can't say I'm surprised. You're coming with us, right? You're not leaving me in the trenches with these newbies?"

"I'm getting too old for this. I just turned fifty, I can't be jumping out of planes and running and gunning anymore."

There was a long pause as Max realized what Jack was asking him to do.

"How much experience do these people have? How old are they?"

"This would be our second assignment as a group, and they're young," Jack said. Taking a deep breath before he continued, he said, "And they were all washouts for various reasons from the FARM."

Letting out a long sigh and looking down at his drink, Max

said, "I'm babysitting. Perfect. What about experience before you recruited them?"

"There was none before—like I said, they're all washouts from the FARM for small reasons, but I saw potential in every one of them. Plus, because they're technically washouts, they won't have anything on file showing that they're part of—"

"The agency making it that much harder to identify them if someone were going to try and hack into the servers. I like the concept of it. It makes a lot of sense, but if I do this, then they take orders from me downrange, no questions. And maybe when this is all said and done, it's a strong maybe, I'll contemplate joining this team."

"I couldn't have asked for anything else," Jack responded.

"Sounds good to me," Max said, flagging down their waitress yet again, only this time it was to get the check. "How bad is the situation I'm walking into?"

"What do you think Max, the world's most dangerous drug lord kidnapped one of my guys using his sicarios, and we have to get him back. I need you to lead them through the trenches, I can't do it anymore," Jack said. His tone told him all he needed to know. "We tracked the SUV to a house in Nogales and have a satellite currently overlooking the location. I sent a couple of your new teammates to intercept them, but shortly before you showed up, one of the guys called me and said they weren't able to get him."

"You don't have any other information?"

"There was an underground passage that was found, and a note that said 'come and get us gringos'," Jack said.

"Perfect."

"Yep, same shit, different day." Both men pushed in their chairs and discussed a few more items in addition to what time to meet at the airport. Giving one last handshake and hug, Jack hoped and prayed Max would give them the edge they needed.

CHAPTER 7

Max met Jack at the airport just after one o'clock in the afternoon. Once both men were safely aboard the Gulfstream 550, the noise from the turbo jet engines filled the plane as it taxied out to the runway. Once they were in the air and had reached their cruising altitude, Jack filled Max in about how the Bering Group operated. When they had finished with the details, there was still about an hour or so left before they landed, so Max decided to catch some sleep. Landing at five-thirty, Max went to collect both their bags as Jack made a phone call to Pete to see if any updates were available.

The ride to Gainesville was quiet. Max spent the time in the passenger seat admiring the different trees and scenery the further they got from the city. Pulling into the subdivision, Jack flashed their IDs to the gate guard, who opened the gate, making a familiar creaking noise reminding Max of the worst horror movie he could think of. The neighborhood was engulfed with so many trees and shrubbery it could be mistaken for a Planet of the Apes movie set, Max was in shock.

"How on Earth did you guys secure funding to live in a neighborhood like this?"

Jack just smiled and left it alone. Making a left onto a side street, he slowed his pace, made another left, and pulled onto the long winding driveway.

"I see you have people that work for you with poor taste in vehicles," Max said, trying to wrap his head around the couple of beaters and one decent-looking SUV. Parking next to the massive bronze water fountain of Poseidon with his trident, Jack killed the engine.

"Don't worry about your bag," Jack said. "I'll get it."

"I get a chauffeur and a bell boy if I work for you? Things are already starting to look up!" Max said, pulling his sunglasses over his face.

"I said I'll get your bag, I didn't say I wouldn't do anything to it, smartass," Jack scoffed.

"Whatever you say, boss."

Shaking his head as he opened the front door, Jack said, "Head upstairs to the theater room, they're all probably in there."

"If I can find it, jeez." He was in awe at the old rustic-looking floor and massive ceilings that seemed to stretch out to eternity.

"Easy, it's upstairs on the top floor, first room on the left."

"Roger," Max said. The house was freshly renovated, yet the wooden stairs squeaked and moaned at every step he made. Finally reaching the top floor, he still couldn't hear anything, but took Jack's advice and opened the door to his left.

He felt as if he stepped into a local bar and, being an outsider, the needle stopped on the record.

"Who's the new guy?" Kyle asked, sitting in his recliner to Max's right.

"I'm the guy they wanted to hire to make sure you do your job," Max said, quickly shutting the door. "You must be the other guy." Giving an annoyed look back, not having anything else to say, Kyle turned back around and pulled out his cell phone.

"Don't worry about him," Kwame said, walking over to him to shake his hand.

"Firm grip there," Max said, ending the handshake and rubbing his right hand.

"It's nice to meet you man, some people," Kwame said, pointing to Kyle, "will take a bit getting used to." Making a little more light conversation with Max, Kwame finished and decided to take the seat next to Kyle. One by one the rest of the team introduced themselves. Max was easily the oldest in the room at thirty-three. Great, he thought.

The last person to introduce themselves was Courtney, who he found incredibly beautiful. Her long hair was tied in a pony-tail extending down to the small of her back. He noticed her the second he entered the room but was abruptly interrupted by the ignorant asshole with the New England accent. This was going to be fun, he thought.

The door opened once more, and Max took a seat in the back next to Kwame as Jack entered the room. Heading to the front, he pulled up the computer and pressed a button to lower the projection screen as the current satellite image of the house in Nogales appeared.

"Okay, first and foremost, I assume everyone has met our newest team member, Max Fontaine?"

"Yes," the group spoke in unison.

"He'll be working with us on this until we find Ben. Treat him with respect and let's not have any issues, got it?"

Everyone nodded in unison.

"Let's jump right into this," he said, turning to address Pete. His skinny figure and wire-rimmed glasses screamed analyst for some major tech company, which couldn't be further from the truth.

"When we searched the house, initially we found nothing. Upon further investigation, Courtney and I found a tunnel discovered behind the wall in the pantry. Of course, we didn't go down the tunnel but nonetheless, it's there. Based on previous narco-trafficking trends, I would suggest that it leads somewhere into Mexico and that's where they took Ben. Janet has her team working on some satellite thermal imagery to try and figure out where it leads, but they have nothing yet." Looking at Jack before continuing with the next part and receiving a nod for a go-ahead, he continued, "There was also the matter of a note left that said, 'come and get us gringos'. This could only mean one thing: there's a mole somewhere in the agency."

Jack let the last part linger in the air before jumping in. "I've encountered this sort of thing in the past, but back then it would have been handled differently—as in truth serum, ropes, cattle prongs, if you get the gist," Jack chuckled. Seeing surprised eyes from everyone except Max, he continued. "Anyway, keep it hush-hush for now until I figure this all out. No mention of the note outside of this room, there's no telling who we can trust now. Not even Janet." Silence fell around the room, but the severity of the situation was understood.

"Adding to Pete," Alex said, drinking from his coffee cup as his right bicep looked like it was going to explode through his t-shirt. "We sat in front of that house for a couple of hours before entering it, and we know for a fact they didn't leave because the SUV was parked in the driveway the entire time."

"How do you know the SUV was at the house the entire time and didn't leave to go somewhere else before you guys got there?" Kyle asked, flicking his long black hair backward trying to prevent it from falling in front of his eyes.

"If you were paying attention, you would have remembered the satellites watching the house," Alex responded, his Puerto Rican accent coming out stronger than he wanted.

"Just asking a question, jeez," Kyle said.

It was then Max decided to say his piece as he walked up to the front of the room. Knowing he was about to address people who he had never worked with and vice versa, he only hoped they would listen to what he had to say. He was sure they were a solid group of individuals, but he knew it was easier said than done sometimes telling people how to operate even if the new guy had more experience.

"Jack, can you pull up a map of Arizona and Mexico for me, please?"

"No problem." Jack minimized the satellite feed and brought up a google map of the border.

"I've spent many assignments south of the border and I can tell you, do not underestimate the expansive network of these tunnels. These are very smart individuals with a lot of money and resources to have us guessing until we die from heat exhaustion as to where each one of their tunnels leads.

"My personal opinion, what they probably did was get out right here," he said, looking at the map and pointing to an area that was about a mile south of the border. "After they got out, they possibly had a vehicle waiting for them and drove to some safe house," he said, looking over at Jack to see if he had any more additional information.

"How long is the drive from the border of Arizona to the Gulf of California?" Kwame asked.

"It's around four-and-a-half hours, give or take, depending on how far south they wanted to drive. I've done that drive myself working undercover a few years back—it's a very long and monotonous drive."

"Is there anything you haven't done?" Courtney asked.

Max looked at Jack and they both laughed. The duo had such a dynamic history together and the team would never know the type of shenanigans they got into working together. "Surprisingly enough, I haven't seen a cock fight." He had the room laughing at this one.

Jack spoke. "Alejandro is a very smart individual and has very specific routes he has his drug runners take when their moving shipments. He doesn't run the most feared cartel in the world for no reason."

"It seems like we have an idea of what they did with Ben, so now I guess we have to come up with some sort of plan?" Nate asked, the only member of the group who was standing in the back of the room. His lean yet muscular six-foot frame screamed CrossFit as he took a swig from his water jug.

Just as Jack was going to answer the question, his pocket vibrated. "It's time, I have to take this." Max gave a final nod as Jack stepped out and shut the door.

The room was silent once more as Max cleared his throat. "I know there's some rumors floating around the agency about myself and what I do and the history I've had here. Right now, you don't need to be concerned with what I did in the past or how I got here or if the rumor mills are true. I'm here as a favor to Jack and you all are the new kids on the block.

"I'm here to make sure things run smoothly and efficiently downrange. If you listen to what I have to say when I say it, they will. Alejandro Alvarez is a mean and dirty son of a bitch and will do anything and everything to make sure we fail. What you did in the past and how you got here doesn't matter anymore, and quite frankly I don't care because when rounds start ricocheting off the trees and walls next to you, all that résumé bullshit goes out the window. Not everybody can last in a two-way range, but I'm here to make sure you can."

Looking around the room, Max could tell they were ready on the outside, but time would tell on the inside. There was silence throughout the room now as Jack walked back inside.

"The authorities have raided that house before and others in that neighborhood because it's known for trafficking illegals into the United States. Our intel guesses they're taking him to an abandoned airfield located in Guaymas, Mexico. Previous intel suggests that there is some sort of hideout close by so that the traffickers can have a place to stay while doing business out there.

"Here's what we're going to do. Max, I want you Courtney and Kwame to head down to Cabo. I have an old contact that's retired Mexican Special Forces. When I know more information, I'll text it to you, but until then, grab your bags and head to the airport. The rest of you, head to the agency and link up with Janet. She says she has a lot of information for you guys to dig through, and instead of her bringing it here it would just be easier for you to cypher through it in one of the conference rooms. She pulled up all the information they have on the Saint Bertrand Cartel and Alejandro. Study it like your lives depended on it."

"Roger that, boss man," Max said. Courtney and Kwame followed Max out of the room and downstairs into the kitchen. Grabbing a cup from the cupboard, he turned to his two new partners. "What about weapons and ammo?" he asked Courtney.

"They're all on the plane already."

"Easy day," he responded.

Max told Courtney and Kwame what time he would meet them at the airport and told them he had some things he had to do at his townhouse first. In the Uber home, all sorts of thoughts were running through his mind. Would he be able to work with these young guys? They seemed nice but if they had only seen a little bit of action, this certainly wouldn't be a walk in the park. He knew that running around anywhere south of the border would put some hair on their chest. As he watched the droves of trees and cars pass him by, he almost wished he had just told Jack *no*. Working for himself was undoubtedly the greatest gift he had ever received, and he just traded it all for babysitting.

The Uber made a right past a busy street full of bars and restaurants and pulled up to the front of his townhouse. Jumping out and thanking the driver, he turned toward the restaurants and took a big whiff of the fresh air. He fought the urge to walk to his favorite bar. Even though he knew everyone working there, and all were great people, there was only one person he really wanted to see: Wendy. This job had always had its complications, and as much as he wanted a relationship—no, as much as he was ready for a relationship, he knew he couldn't have one. She had been flirting with him ever since she was hired two months ago, but he had never even asked for her number. Maybe if he joined Jack's team, there might be a chance. He walked up the stairs and put his key into the lock.

Looking at his Omega Seamaster, he knew he only had an hour before he had to meet his new teammates at the airport. It was just enough time. He hurried upstairs to his bedroom, dropped his clothes, and hopped in the shower. Time flew by. He packed what he needed to, not knowing exactly how long he would be gone.

Standing at the door to his place and taking one last browse, he was satisfied. It looked as if it were just pulled straight out of a magazine. All in all, he wasn't that much of a neat freak; it had just been a while since he had spent time here. He turned and headed to the garage.

Clicking on the light switch, Max set his bag on the ground and walked over to the vehicle sitting underneath the black car cover. A slow feeling of euphoria swept across his face and down through his body as the small Porsche logo stared back at him. Beginning at the front, he walked the length of the car, pulling off the car cover and exposing a brand-new Porsche Cayman GT4 he purchased two years ago. Setting the cover on the counter and placing his bags in the hood of the car—Europeans are so weird, he thought—he closed the hood and slid into the pristine tan interior. He opened the garage door and put the key into the ignition. The engine roared to life. The only girl in his life right now was excited to take him on his next adventure. He looked at the time—he had thirty minutes to make it to the airport. Whatever he thought, they weren't leaving without him. Backing out of the driveway, he clicked the garage door closed and raced up the street to rendezvous with his new team.

CHAPTER 8

The pantry passageway emptied out into the bathroom of an abandoned gas station two miles into Mexico. The combination of the mildew-infested sack placed over his head and the extremely long car ride caused Ben to dry heave numerous times in the back of the vehicle. If they had a fuel-efficient car, they could make the drive in over eight hours to Guaymas. However, they were driving a gas-guzzling SUV and—coupled with excessive amount of bathroom breaks—they made it to their destination in just under ten.

It was around lunch time by the time they pulled up to the stash house. Alejandro had connections everywhere including ones in the local police department. The long drive had all four men exhausted and hungry, and left Ben very confused as to what was going on.

The sunlight creeping through the small holes of the sack was his only clue. Wishing he had more situational awareness when he was in San Diego, he couldn't help but think of Bri. His parents were worried sick, he was sure of it, but if the worst was to happen, he knew the agency would deny all possibilities that he was kidnapped by some sort of drug cartel. He would just wind up another star on their infamous memorial wall of lost-but-never-forgotten agents who passed onto the next life while in the field.

He heard his door opening, and one of the sicarios yanked on his right arm, pulling him out of his seat. Not seeing where he was going and trying not to stumble, he was pushed forward. Ben moved his head from left to right to find his surroundings as he tried to remember his survival training, but it was hopeless.

His feet ran right into some steps, and he fell forward and tried to brace his fall with his arms. One of the sicarios caught him.

"It's okay, *cabrón,*" Matias said, "we won't let anything happen to you."

"I'm so sure," Ben said sarcastically. Laughing from all three sicarios fueled his rage to escape and only made him hate them even more. But if they were laughing, then maybe he could strike up a casual conversation and catch one of them slipping on useful information.

CHAPTER 9

Max sat in the back of the C-130 cargo plane alongside Courtney and Kwame. He wanted to take the Gulfstream again, but Jack vetoed it the second he brought it up. For official business ventures they weren't necessarily authorized to use it quite yet. Fuel was a bitch to pay for.

They had a four-and-a-half-hour flight time from Virginia to Cabo San Lucas, and since Jack didn't have any more amplifying information before they boarded, they couldn't do anything but come up with a rough draft of a plan. This took all of twenty minutes, and within thirty after they were airborne, both of his partners were fast asleep. Looking to his right at Kwame, who had an eye mask on, he couldn't help but laugh.

He stood up to stretch a bit and walked over to the gear tied down toward the back of the plane. He certainly missed commercial plane rides serving him alcoholic beverages under the name Daryl Hopkins, but that was a different life. Kneeling and unzipping his bag, he examined their standardized gear. The good news was the Bering Group was the agency's most secretive possession, meaning they had access to all the newest gizmos and gadgets just like Special Forces. He grabbed his silenced MK18 out of the bag, pulled the bolt back and, ensuring there was no ammunition in the chamber, pointed it toward the ceiling.

He was used to working with modified M4's, so having the ability to use the MK18 was right up his alley. A 10.3inch Cold Hammer Forged Barrel, able to be used in close quarters battle situations, sporting an Aimpoint optic and canted 45 degree angle iron sights fit the bill perfectly. He loved it. His left thumb slid over a small button on an attachment to the side of the firearm, producing a faint green light. It worked. Looking down the front sights and slowing his breathing, he remembered the dry fire drills his dad used to prepare him before they hunted deer in the winter. Careful not to move the entire gun and focusing on his grip, he slid the selector lever off safe and depressed the trigger. The firearm made a clicking noise.

"Slow is smooth, smooth is fast, right?" Courtney said from behind, startling him. Moving his right thumb over the selector lever and putting the weapon on safe, he packed it back inside the bag.

"Yup," Max said. "What's your backstory, Courtney?"

"Call me Court. Nobody calls me Courtney—my parents only call me that when they're upset." Max laughed.

"I can relate. My full name is Maximillian, but I went by Max growing up. My childhood friends called me by my full name when they wanted to make fun of me," he said.

"Why would they make fun of you? It's a beautiful name."

"What black man do you know named Maximillian?"

Laughing, she said, "Okay, I see your point."

"What am I going to do, go back in time and water board my parents until they change my name?"

"Have you seen some of the names parents come up with these days? It's like, what the hell were you thinking?"

"That's just it, they weren't," Max said, smiling.

Courtney gazed over the gear, then back at Kwame, who was still fast asleep. She continued, "Anyway, after the FARM was over—"

"I don't care about the training. Tell me about your personal life," Max said.

"I grew up in Pontiac, Michigan, thirty minutes outside of Detroit. I have a mom, dad, and two older brothers. My dad owns a construction business, and my mom is a college professor," she stated.

"Interesting combination."

"I guess," she said, walking over and leaning on the bulkhead. "I did gymnastics in high school and was picked on by the other girls because I was always skinnier than everyone else."

"Picked on? I didn't see that one coming," Max said, walking over to hear her better over the four engines groaning outside.

She continued. "My brothers always wrestled with each other and were on the wrestling team all throughout middle school and into high school, so they helped me out. I enjoyed it, plus the other girls stopped picking on me after I got into a little tussle and broke one of their arms with an armbar."

Max winced.

"I graduated high school, became a bartender in Detroit for about a year. Saw enough crime around me to write a book about it. I always hated people who committed crimes and was always trying to help the bouncers throw people out of the bars when they acted up, so the manager suggested I become a cop and do something with my life. I talked to my parents about it, and they said I should start college and try to get a federal job with benefits, yah know?"

"You applied to the CIA, failed out, and were recruited by Jack who happened to see something inside of you."

"Bingo," she said.

Max nodded. "You're an attractive woman," he said, seeing her blush and smiling at the compliment. "What's the dating life like with this schedule Jack keeps you guys on?"

Her loving expression quickly faded away as she looked at the ground. "Sometimes it's not easy, especially with someone who's outside of the community."

Max could tell something was bothering her. "Sorry, if I struck a nerve."

Looking back at him, she said, "No, it's fine. I just caught my current boyfriend talking to his ex."

Just as she was about to continue, the door to the cockpit opened. The co-pilot's height forced him to duck, as he walked through the door frame, waving Max over.

"It seems we'll have to pick this up at another time," he said. Jack sure wasn't kidding when he Courtney said was something else to look at. Although she mentioned her boyfriend, he also was curious as to where Jack stood on dating. But he could figure that out another time.

Following the co-pilot through the door and closing it behind him, he walked up to the two chairs and put his arms around them both. The co-pilot grabbed his chair, put on his headset, and signaled to the pilot he had control, striking up a conversation with Max. After shoving Max back a couple of feet so he had some space to get up, he sighed and crossed his arms. "Jack wants me to tell you there's been a slight change of plans."

"How slight?" Max said with concern.

"He said his boy you're supposed to get in contact with is ready to roll on the ground and has four other men with him, which is the good news."

"The bad?"

"He also wants you guys to do a hot drop."

Now it all made sense, Max thought. A last-minute decision in the air to parachute onto a target—nobody liked having to do it. Jumping out of a moving plane was hard enough, sure, but people liked to pack their own parachutes and psych themselves up for a jump. The altitude didn't matter when it came to a hot drop; the only difference was whether an oxygen mask was required.

"How high are we dropping?" he asked, now pulling out a notepad to scribble everything down for his teammates.

"Around twenty-five thousand," the pilot said, "and he also said to look for a bright red boat with the word *Zulu* written in white on top of the pilothouse."

"That's funny," Max said.

"I don't get the joke," said the pilot.

"That's the codename Jack and I were given when we worked together as a team back in the day. It made it easier for the superiors to track everyone down range, and we didn't tell a whole lot of people outside of our circle for obvious reasons."

The pilot handed Max a piece of paper with the name of the captain of the Special Forces and his exact GPS coordinates in black ink. "The parachutes and oxygen tanks are lined up on the left bulkhead. There's ten in total so pick and choose which ones you guys want to use; Lord knows we don't care."

Nodding, Max said, "Is that it?"

"He said everything was sorted out and his friend would give you the details when you guys linked up. It sounds like you guys have a long day ahead of you. I'll let you know when we're thirty mikes out. When we're five mikes I'll kill the lights in the bay and the red—"

"I got it, done these enough times. Thanks, brother," Max said. The pilot gave a thumbs-up and sat back in his chair. Max took a good look at the weather through the windshield. It was nothing but blue skies with no clouds as far as the eye could see. Perfect weather, he thought. Although he knew all too well that Murphy's Law was in hibernation, waiting for the right time to wake up.

CHAPTER 10

After inspecting their parachutes individually, they each passed them off to someone else to do a double check. They needed to keep Murphy at bay; after all, this was only the beginning to what Max was sure to be a long journey ahead. When the inspections were complete, they looked over their gear once more, ensuring their weapons dry-fired perfectly, plate carriers fit properly, and oxygen bottles were at max capacity. Next came the coordinates, which Max had plugged into everyone's GPS beacon earlier and strapped to their individual arms in case they were separated.

"Well," Kwame said, "this will be fun."

Courtney rotated her forearm and studied the digital map. "It looks like this location is around nine or so miles from Cabo San Lucas," she said, tapping the device and using her fingers to expand the view.

Sitting back and thinking a second, Max said, "That's actually perfect. Too far away to be spotted from wandering eyes off the coast, but not too far off either."

"That's going to be a hell of a swim if we get separated," Kwame said.

"Then don't get separated, big boy," Max said with a grin.

"Five mikes out," said a booming voice over the intercom. The lights went out and the frigid air swept through the cargo bay as the ramp lowered. The wool layers in addition to the flight suit were not nearly enough to keep Max from shivering.

Placing their helmets on, each member attached parachutes to their gear bags connected to a timer synched with each person's individual chute on their backs. The gear bags would go first, followed by the operators not far behind. They made their way to the edge of the ramp quickly, tightening their straps and conducting one last helmet communications check as they grabbed the remaining gear.

"Everyone, sync your watches in three... two... one... now," Max said from his helmet. The helmet was the equivalent of a thin full face motorcycle helmet with a heads-up display, the newest edition to their Gucci gear line.

"Roger."

Sixty seconds. Looking at his watch, he watched the second hand glide around its frame effortlessly. He couldn't help but think about his entire life had led him up to this. Max had gone through a lot, not as a child per se, but with his career. He had teamed up with Jack for years and accomplished so much and learned a lot working with him. Jack had developed him into the man and operator he was today. As much as he loved working solo, he did enjoy the banter between the team. It kept things from getting too lonely.

Forty-five seconds. He didn't think he was going to want a higher-paying position in the agency, but if he accepted, a bonus would definitely be involved. The truth of the matter was, he was fine working for Jack, and this crew was definitely growing on him.

Thirty seconds. Max waved his hands forward as they trudged to the edge of the ramp. Flashbacks to childhood, what he could have done or where he could have ended up always seemed to make a mental stand at pivotal moments like these in his mind. Not knowing why didn't bother him; he just accepted it.

"Standby! In three... two... one... Go!" He waited until both Kwame and Courtney ran past him, then he leapt right behind them, accelerating toward the open ocean. Max ensured he wasn't more than five paces behind Kwame, pushing his bag off the ramp and making a big X with his body. Thanks to the suit, Max was impervious to the freezing air—but he still hated being in the cold.

Glancing at his HUD, the digital altimeter displayed twenty-three thousand feet.

That's when he noticed it.

The biggest threat Max remembered from class was an uncontrollable spin, where blood would rush to the extremities, including the head, causing temporary blindness. The force of the spin coupled with the blood rush to the head could cause massive bleeding in the brain and clotting would ensue, meaning death. That's what Max was witnessing with Court's jump.

"Standby, Court, I'm coming!" Kwame shouted, forming a thin-like pencil shape as he tilted his body downward to increase his velocity.

"Right behind you," Max said, copying Kwame's figure and picking up speed himself.

"Court! Court!"

"I think she's passed out already!"

"Kwame, fan out now or you're going to shoot past her!" Max shouted, but it was too late. Coming in way too fast, Kwame tried to grab Courtney but blew past her right side. It was all up to Max now. Approaching Court, he fanned out himself and looked at HUD. Just above twenty thousand feet.

He crashed into Courtney and wrapped his entire body around her, his momentum matching her speed and trying to stop her body from the flat spin. Her eyes were shut. Reaching just to the right of her chest, he felt the chord to the parachute and ripped it as hard as he could. The chute and stabilizer flew upwards, slowing down their decent. The problem wasn't over, though, because he was still attached to her and the extra weight was causing them to fall faster than what the parachute was weighted for.

Courtney was still unconscious, the HUD now reading sixteen-thousand feet. Max reached over, created a fist, and rubbed excessively on her sternum. Nothing.

"Kwame, I need you to track Courtney's bag, we just shot past it."

"On it!" he said, pulling his own chute to try and stay together as best he could.

"Come on Court," Max said, his HUD displaying numbers falling too fast. Fumbling for her front zipper, he reached through and maneuvered his right hand through her under-layers until he was sure he felt skin. He rubbed so hard on her sternum he was sure the skin was becoming one with his glove.

After a few seconds of intense rubbing, her eyes snapped open.

Regaining her surroundings and seeing Max's hand in her shirt, she said, "Listen, I still have a boyfriend."

Yanking his hand away and frowning, Max shoved off right at ten thousand feet, but stayed as close as possible to monitor her.

"You good, Court?" Kwame asked, trying to tilt his head up, barely able to make out his teammates.

"Yeah man, I'm good," she replied, "just a little dizzy is all." Trying her best to focus on Max, her vision slowly returning back to normal.

"I thought we lost you back there," Max said.

"I was just testing you," she replied, giving a thumbs-up.

"I hate to interrupt, guys, but I spy with my little eye a contact bearing zero-five-four," Kwame said, using his big right arm to point into the distance. Luckily the fiasco in the air didn't blow them too far off-course, putting them only half a mile or so away from their boat.

The rest of their decent went by smoothly and the second they hit the water, a balloon capable of holding their weight and stuffed with a small CO_2 canister erupted on their belts. The warm weather and water were kind of relaxing to Max, even though he knew he was now on the bottom of the oceanic food chain until the boat picked them up. Nonetheless, he enjoyed the brief rest as their target made its way closer to them.

CHAPTER 11

"**W**elcome to Mexico," the grey-haired Hispanic gentleman said after he helped Max and the rest of the team out of the water. Enrique Suarez's scraggly salt and pepper hair, which matched his stubble, took on a five o'clock shadow around the lower part of his face. He looked extremely fit for his age. Whatever he was doing during retirement was suiting him nicely. After offering them each a towel and a bottle of water, Enrique grabbed their parachutes and flight suits and gave them to his men to toss in the corner of the boat.

After the proper greetings were exchanged, they went inside to what little space they had for a kitchen. The boat was only forty-seven feet long and looked like every other fishing boat in Southern Pacific. Running rust was prevalent around the entire outside of the vessel, the smell of rotten fish everywhere they stepped. The operators on the boat continuously ducked and dodged low-hanging wires, a reoccurring theme throughout the vessel.

"You know, I could almost mistake this for an actual drug boat," Max said, standing in the corner of the small kitchen, leaning against one of the rusted-out pipes.

"That's because it probably is. We stole it." Enrique laughed. "We didn't have a non-conspicuous boat to pick you guys up in," he said, cocking his head to the side thinking of another vessel they possibly could have taken. "Alright," Enrique said, looking around at all the individuals crowded in the kitchen. "First things first. You three," he said, pointing to the Americans that parachuted into the water, "y'all need to understand that the Mexican cartel owns Guaymas, but they share it with the Saint Bertrand Cartel." His heavy Mexican accent lingered in the air.

"How does the Saint Bertrand Cartel share this area if it's in Mexico?" Courtney asked, taking a sip from her water bottle.

"Let me correct myself, they own some of the property down here but, because they 'lease' some of the buildings," he said with finger quotes, "they helped to pay the cartel down here to pretty much buy out *la policia*," Enrique said, then taking a swig from his own water bottle. Snapping his fingers and signaling to one of his men, he said something in Spanish. The guy he spoke to stepped back outside, not entering the kitchen again. "Second thing you guys need to realize, we're in Mexican waters. We're only ten miles out, which means that we're not quite in international waters however, every boat out here is considered a drug boat—"

"Meaning that we have a high potential to be stopped and boarded like everyone else being we're still in state waters," Max said.

"Bingo, my friend," Enrique replied. "We're on our own out here, not to mention again that this boat is stolen. Now I hope nobody gets seasick, because from here we have a decently long trek inside the inflatable boats we have covered up in the back." He pointed to the area on the fantail covered in tarps.

"What about this boat?" Kwame asked, feeling queasy.

"You alright, amigo?" one of Enrique's men asked, as he put his arm on his shoulder.

"I'm fine, I was just never a fan of the open ocean, I just need to—" he stopped mid-sentence and ran outside.

"We're going to anchor this boat here," Enrique said. The man who had stepped outside, presumably to keep a lookout, had now peeked his head through the threshold and said something in quick Spanish that neither Max nor his partners could make out.

Enrique turned toward his new friends and, seeing their bags piled into one corner on the boat, said, "Tell me you have silencers to accompany all that gear?" Not needing to say anymore, Max walked over, Courtney doing the same, and opened the watertight zipper, pulling out their gear to show Enrique. Satisfied with what he was looking at, he said, "I hope you gringos brought your A-game, because you may need it sooner rather than later. We have a boat approaching us, it'll be here in twenty so get ready."

"You three don't speak Spanish, do you?" Enrique asked as Kwame stepped back in the room, having remnants of spit on his shirt.

"We can get by," Max said, picking up on the fact that they should hide so they avoid questioning.

"Typically they just want us to answer a couple of quick questions but if they step onto this boat, they don't step back off. The local enforcement is all corrupt, so they will waste no time in notifying their cartel friends they have some unwelcome visitors from up North."

"Just more victims of the drug war," Max said, handing Kwame his pistol and silencer attachment.

Finishing his talk, Enrique told the rest of his men who were still inside to walk back outside. Following suit, he told the three to sit tight and went outside to greet the oncoming two speedboats.

CHAPTER 12

Pete, Alex, Kyle, and Nate had been sitting with Janet in the seventh-floor conference room, with Davids approval, for several hours. Alejandro's cartel was more extensive than any of them had imagined, and his empire spread to several corners of the globe. They had their hands in everything from drugs, illegal sex trafficking, and even running a series of casinos throughout various Indian reservations in the United States. Alejandro Alvarez was clearly a very smart and savvy individual. Janet and the team covered all of Alejandro's financial records, possible hideouts, drug routes, and every other aspect that dealt with his powerful cartel.

"Fuck," Nate said, stacking the last bit of papers together neatly, then putting them with the rest of the pile in the middle of the table. "I think I have enough information to start and run my own cartel."

"Oh really?" Kyle said, "and what are you going to call it? *Gringos R' Us?*"

Snickering ensued as Nate flipped Kyle the bird.

"You idiots wouldn't know the first thing about running a drug cartel," Alex said who was sitting with his back toward the table. He was flipping through the television channels even though they were all muted.

"Oh, and you do?" Kyle replied, his arms crossed and leaning back in his chair. "Listen, just because you're Puerto Rican doesn't mean you know any more than we do, bro."

Without skipping a beat, Alex replied, "I know more than you do gringo, you grew up in Iowa." Nate and Pete roared out with laugher.

"Bro, you grew up in the suburbs of New Mexico and was born into oil money. You're no better than me," Kyle said. "Like I said, just because you're Hispanic doesn't mean you know any more than me when it comes to this crap."

"I never said that I know any more than you, I just said you gringos wouldn't know the first thing about trafficking drugs."

Kyle looked over at Nate and Pete, who both shook their heads. "It's true," Pete said.

Standing up from his chair and walking over to the window, producing of the best views in the building, Kyle paused to think. The spectacular evergreen trees sporting the sea of green for miles was a picture meant for a Hallmark postcard.

"Who's gonna get Janet?" Alex asked, his head now on the table with his eyes closed.

"The real question is, did you guys see that girl who works in cyber security?" Nate asked, sparking a new conversation piece for the room. Kyle turned around and responded, "Dude, I did, I think her name is Alexandria. How old do you think she is?"

"It doesn't matter, we all know she's not into boys with toys the size of my pinky," Alex replied, holding up his pinky finger and flexing it in exaggeration. Pete and Nate laughed again.

"Will you both shut up," Kyle said. "Yeah, she's attractive but I meant to tell you guys, when I used the bathroom about two hours ago, she pulled me aside and talked to me for a bit."

"Nice, bro, I'll find you a lawyer for when she slaps you with a restraining order for being a creep. But don't worry, I hear attorneys give discounts to idio—" Nate said, but caught a dry-eraser to the side of the head from Kyle before he finished his sentence.

"Listen, clowns, what I'm saying is she came off flirtatious, but then dove into some questions about the operation," Kyle said.

"What do you mean?" Alex asked, lifting his head and giving Kyle his undivided attention.

"I'm saying, we may have accumulated all the information we can about the Saint Bertrand Cartel, but remember what Jack said about the rat?"

"Hold on, bro," Nate said, standing up across the table from Kyle. "Jack said there was he thinks there's a rat, but we can't just jump to conclusions every time someone asks us what we're doing here. I mean think about it, for most of the time we're at the office, so when we're in this building, people are naturally going to be a little curious. If I worked here I would know whose who, it only makes sense."

"I know, man, but still, something to think about." Pete said, arms crossed as silence fell throughout the room. Just then the door opened as Janet peeked her head inside.

"You guys all solid?" she asked, receiving blank looks throughout the room. "Did I interrupt something? Or is that just your 'here comes that bitch Janet' expression?" That opened them up.

The team didn't necessarily hate her, they just disliked her because Jack didn't like her. All in all, she was very kind to them throughout the day and even threw in some jabs at the men to help ease the stress of looking at the same files all day long. No, Jack could hate Janet all he wanted to, but the four men inside the room found her very attractive and neither one of them minded a little eye candy.

Pete grabbed the stack of papers, photos, and the flash drive sitting in the middle of the glass table and handed them to her. Janet stepped into the room to grab everything, dressed in yoga pants and a light blue tank top, attracting the eyes of all four individuals.

Looking back up at Pete, her hands full, she said, "Thanks boys, I appreciate the help going through all this stuff."

"No problem," said the team.

"You gonna need us tomorrow?" Alex asked, who was standing up now, but turned around to shut the television off.

"No, you guys are golden. Just report to Jack at the Office, I think he said he wants you guys doing close quarters battle drills at the training site for the rest of the week." Jack's motto was, "do what you need to do, then you can do what you want to do." He constantly embedded it inside all members of the Bering Group.

"Any word on the rest of the crew?" Kyle asked.

"We got confirmation they made their jump from the pilot, but that was it," she said, closing the door.

"Sweet, beers, gents?" Kyle asked.

"I'm down, but what about the Alexandria situation?" Pete replied.

"I don't think anybody needs to say anything just yet. Janet and David can't know what we're thinking, and not only will they both think we're crazy, but they're going to want more evidence that their cyber security supervisor is prodding for information in an agency that deals with counterintelligence." Nate said.

"What, we just tell Jack?" Kyle questioned.

"Wouldn't hurt. He always says what's discussed within the walls of the office stays within the walls. Plus, it'll give him a person to prod," Alex responded. "Now, enough work talk, let's go get those beers."

CHAPTER 13

The two twenty-foot response boats were closing in and now five minutes out from reaching the side of the fishing vessel. Max, Courtney, and Kwame were sitting inside the disgusting kitchen as the rest of the ex-Mexican special force's operators were outside playing the role of stubborn fisherman that didn't want to be interrupted from their work. They had the fishing poles, bait, and whatever other gear they needed to match the part. Even though the ex-military members were out of the game for quite some time, they were not fans of the local authorities or anyone else who had ties to any kind of drug cartel.

The perfect placement for the team was discussed so that if shots were fired from the outside, nobody sitting on the inside of the boat would become a casualty. Entering the cabin, directly to the right was Max and Courtney leaning against the bulkhead just a couple feet apart, with Kwame standing to the left.

Enrique gave a quick rundown to his new friends with how the inspections were handled when they boarded a vessel. There were two boats—one was a protective boat where the members just sat watching the crew outside, while the other boat's team boarded and asked the questions. Under no circumstances were Max and his team to be found; however, because there were two boats approaching and Enrique's men couldn't see exactly how many people were on the boats, they also didn't want to be out-manned and outgunned in case things took a turn for the worst. Enrique instructed Max and his team to just hide and if anyone stepped into the cabin, it was fair game to light them up. After all, they were corrupt. When Courtney asked what would happen when a couple of law enforcement officers didn't return to their post, or their boats for that matter, she received laughs from all of Enrique's men. She took the hint.

Ten minutes went by as Max and the team heard the hum of the gas-powered Yamaha engines pulling alongside. Getting into their positions, he looked over at Kwame and gave him a thumbs-up to which he responded the same. Still showing faint signs of seasickness, he tilted his head back to rest it on the wall. Conducting a quick peek around the corner, Max was able to get a glimpse of the boarding team.

"AKs, at least two heads per boat, maybe three," Max whispered to Courtney and Kwame. In the next couple of minutes, they heard an exchange of words and people jumping over the railing onto their fishing vessel. Hearing footsteps coming closer to the cabin, he saw Courtney, who was left-handed, unholster her pistol. Max looked at her and mouthed the word *relax* as a bead of sweat rolled down his forehead and hung off the tip of his nose.

"Señor, follow me, I can grab whatever you and your men need. Can I offer you three some water?" Enrique asked.

Hearing the footsteps come closer to the cabin, Max took long and steady breaths to help control his breathing. Enrique was the first to enter the cabin and kept walking straight up the stairs to the pilot house, leading the boarding team behind him to their immediate death.

Max waited until all three men walked past him before making his move. Wasting no time, he pulled the trigger as two Springfield XD nine-millimeter rounds penetrated his target, ripping the brain tissue apart and sending a massive coagulation of blood out the back of the skull. The smell of gun powder and noise from the shell casings hitting the deck filled the room as Kwame and Courtney finished dropping their targets. Almost instantly, loud noises were heard from outside in conjunction with what was going on inside the cabin, and then, silence.

"Is it clear?" Enrique shouted from above in the pilothouse.

"All clear!" Max shouted, holstering his pistol.

Walking up to Max's target, Kwame looked down at the two small holes sitting just above the bridge of the nose and said, "No love was lost on yours."

"That's the price they pay," Max said. "Coming out!"

Stepping outside, he saw three men slumped in different areas of the boat. Enrique's men had already begun tying all three bodies up with whatever weights they could find to get them ready to be tossed over the side.

"Good job, guys," Enrique said, following Max and his team outside. "It won't be long before they're hailed on the radio, so we have to beat feet out of this area and sink those boats." And with that, all operators on the boat went to work.

The sky turned to a reddish-orange hue as the sun sank into the ocean's horizon. Enrique took two of his men and shot a couple of small holes into the deck of both response boats and tied up the dead bodies around the engines. He hopped back on the fishing boat as water began seeping through and sailed away. The GPS coordinates being fed to their main office would not show anything of significance other than that two boats were assumed to be doing some kind of boarding out in the ocean. By the time the coordinates would stop pinging, the boats would already be down in the bottom of Davy Jones's locker.

Dinner was MRE's provided by Enrique and his men. As the moon crept into view in the night sky, the team finished their meals and stepped back outside to look at the schematic of the safe house that cartel operated out of when they wanted to move their product.

"Alright," Enrique said, who had a schematic of the compound where he was more than certain they were holding Ben, "let's do this." Unraveling a rolled-up poster-sized satellite image of the compound, he laid it on one of the empty fuel drums. "The compound is sitting directly on the beach overlooking the Gulf of California, and it's a two-story building that sits at around twenty-four hundred square feet. There's a large black steel fence that surrounded the property except of course around the back which has access to the beach.

"There's no guard shacks, but there was roving security last I checked. Alejandro wanted it to appear to the naked eye that it was just another beachfront property owned by some rich person, although every local person knows who the house belongs to. In an hour or so, as soon as night falls, we'll make the trek into the mouth of the Gulf in the inflatable boats underneath that tarp," Enrique said, pointing to a spot on the map half a mile away from the compound. "From here, Max, Courtney, Kwame, myself and you, Matthew, will make the trek along the beach to the far fence... here." Once again, moving his fingers along the beach line to where the fence surrounded the compound.

"After you guys get off," said Roberto, the man standing to Enrique's right, "I, Sanchez and Mateo will back the boats out into the Gulf and stay one hundred yards offshore ready for extract." There was silence as everyone studied the plan and ran through countless scenarios that could possibly happen during an operation like this. Max rubbed his hands through his beard before asking his first question. "Where are the evac points? Obviously, we have the primary, which I'm guessing is the beach." He pointed to the back of the compound. "But where do we go after that and what if we can't get to it?"

"Yes, the beach will be primary, and once we're scooped up, we'll make the trek to my AirBnB I rent out in Cabo to little American vacationers. It's right on the beach and anyone looking for you guys won't expect you to be there. Secondary, we'll figure it out if it comes to that."

"You don't have a secondary point of evac?" Max asked, confused that someone of his stature would risk everything for a mission like this and not have a backup plan.

"Are you nervous?" Enrique asked with a smirk.

"No secondary? We're serving ourselves up to Murphy on a silver platter," Max stated, clearly frustrated now.

Unfolding his arms and leaning back on the table, Enrique stared at Max long and hard before replying.

"And beating him at his own game is what we all train for, amigo, is it not?"

CHAPTER 14

Just after the sun set beyond the horizon, the sicarios held a conversation with the roving security replacing the earlier shift of guards. Pablo decided to keep Ben locked away in one of the spare bedrooms upstairs, far enough away from any traffic coming and going throughout the house. When the guards swapped, Pablo went into the living room, turned off the television, and walked over to his partners pouring tequila and clearing the dinner table to play a game of dominoes. Opening the refrigerator, he grabbed three glasses and a baby monitor relayed to Ben's room and sat down at the head of the table. A couple of hours remained before making the twenty-minute drive to the abandoned air strip in the middle of the rainforest.

Looking through the night vision goggles sitting just in front of his eyes, Enrique pointed at the bottom floor of the right side of the building. The columns of floor-to-ceiling windows with no blinds made it easy to see inside the house. The group sat just a hundred yards away from the house, bobbing and weaving with the gentle current. At that distance they were invisible to the naked eye. Looking through his own NVGs, Max was able to spot a handful of armed guards walking around the outside of the house, and prayed a small army wasn't waiting for them inside.

The light from a door upstairs illuminated the balcony outside as a guard stepped out and the one outside replaced him inside the house. Max watched as the new guard propped his rifle against the house and took a seat in the rocking chair at the end of the balcony.

"It looks like security is pretty relaxed," Max said, lifting his goggles, tilting his head backward and looking at the stars illuminating the sky. He always said the best nights were out at sea.

"Watch this," Enrique said as he pulled out what looked like a small radio transmitter with an antenna.

"What's that?" Kwame asked, leaning over Enrique's shoulder watching him playing with the new gadget he was holding.

"It cuts the power to anything it's pointed at, good for thirty minutes. The only downside is they'll for sure know we're coming," he said, hitting one of the few buttons on the small black box which emitted a small beeping noise and displayed a green light on the top right corner. Just seconds after the button was pressed, the lights illuminating from inside of the house went dark.

"Alright, we're good. Stay frosty, fellas—and lady," Enrique said, looking over at Max and his squad who were laying prone on the bow of the other inflatable. Responding through their NVGs and adjusting his shoulders forward to better fit his plate carrier, Max grunted and yawned. It had been an extremely long day. Leaning forward, he pointed his silenced rifle in the direction of the house and prayed to God that Ben was somewhere in that building.

The room inside the house adjacent to where the men were playing dominoes was the security booth. Inside was a wall of numerous televisions and electronics linked to the cameras facing the outside of the property. It was here the security guard watching the cameras noticed something strange on the water. Once it was dark enough, thermal imaging automatically kicked in for all the cameras which allowed any guards watching the screen to see well beyond the beach. The guard called out to Pablo, who was not happy getting up from the game he just sat down for. Stumbling into the security room, he said, "*¿Qué pasó?*"

"I can't figure out what that is," the guard said, leaning as close to the screen as possible. Pablo leaned closer to the screen to see two small figures floating in the middle of the water.

"Matias! Santiago!" Pablo shouted, using the keyboard to zoom into the image.

"What is it?" Matias asked, with his tequila glass in his hand. Pablo backed away and pointed at the forty-inch television display.

"What the—" But Matias was never able to finish his sentence before the entire house was drained of power.

"Dammit, grab the gringo," Pablo said.

"Shit, the breaker just needs to be reset probably," Santiago said, standing behind Matias and downing the rest of his drink.

Pablo pushed past Matias and was now so close to Santiago he could smell the liquor on his breath. "*Pendejo!* Grab the gringo, now!"

"Okay, okay!" replied Santiago, leaving the room.

"You going to call him?" Matias asked, running his hand through his slicked-back hair.

"We have no time," Pablo said, stepping out of the room. "Go get the SUVs ready to go," he told Matias after stepping out. Pablo grabbed a radio sitting on the kitchen counter and pressed the push-to-talk button on the side. "Be on alert everyone, they're coming for their friend," he said, throwing the radio on the kitchen table and walking back into the security booth.

The guard in the booth was now standing and trying to get the systems back online, but nothing was working. Pablo rested his arm on the guard's shoulder and said, "Don't worry. Saint Bertrand will be with you." Grabbing one of the AK's sitting on the table, he wished the guard good luck and to call him with any updates. Grabbing Matias and stepping out of the room, he knew whoever was in the boat was going to overrun the house. The guards had minimal training and it wasn't a coincidence the power went out when they noticed two figures on the water. Pablo did not want to die or have to explain to Alejandro why they lost their prisoner. This would most certainly mean death anyway if Ben got away.

Pushing open the front door, he saw the two SUVs with a couple men in the first, but the only person he could see inside the second SUV was Matias with the windows rolled down. Walking up to his vehicle, he opened the back door and peered inside, but not seeing Santiago or Ben made his blood boil.

"Where is Santiago?!" he snarled.

"*No se*," Matias said. "Last I remember he was grabbing the gringo like you told him."

Pablo pulled his head back outside of the SUV and rubbed his forehead. This was going to be a long night, he thought, as he turned back to head inside the house.

"Be careful, make sure you identify your targets. Last thing we need is to smoke our boy in the face," Max whispered through his throat mic. Running softly on the beach, they approached the rear of the house, their guns at the ready. The floor to ceiling windows left lots of room for the team to be exposed from inside the house, however with the power out, moving to the back doors was a breeze.

"That was easy," Courtney said from the rear of the train.

They formed a small line on the left of the back door. "Hmm," Max whispered, looking through the glass with his NVGs. "I'm not seeing anything inside the house."

"I wonder where all the guards went that we saw earlier," Kwame said.

"Probably getting ready to welcome us with open arms," Enrique snickered. Just as Max was about to check the door handle in front of him, Courtney said, "Wait. I hear something from the front."

"Okay, standby," Max whispered, "I think there's somebody above us." The train sat in silence as the wooden balcony squeaked and moaned underneath the boots of whoever was walking around above them.

"Roberto, do you see anything?" Enrique whispered over the mic.

"Yes, there's two men with rifles. I don't think they know you guys are below them. They're just looking around at the beach but be careful because their rifles are raised."

"Roger," Enrique responded. "Move to the front, very slowly," Max whispered, as Courtney now took point, and the team turned the opposite direction.

Pablo ran back inside and took the stairs nearly three steps at a time heading for the room where Ben was. Not really knowing what to expect, he pulled his pistol out and kicked the door nearly off its hinges. The only thing that was in the room besides the bed was Ben. "Fuck," he said under his breath as he reached into his pocket and dialed Matias, who picked up on the first ring.

"What?"

"Come in here and find Santiago. I have the prisoner."

"You don't see him?" he asked.

"*Puto*, if I saw him would I be calling you? Now hurry up, I'm giving you thirty seconds from when I hang up this phone and if you're not back outside, then I'm leaving you here." He slammed the flip phone shut and put it back in his pocket. Before grabbing Ben off the bed, Pablo put the muzzle to Ben's forehead and said, "*Gringo,* I like you and you haven't been causing us trouble but if you try anything right now, I'll shoot you myself."

"You guys like me?" Ben replied through his burlap sack. He could smell the cigarettes coming from Pablo's breath as he sat limp on the chair, waiting for his wrists and ankles to be untied.

Hearing footsteps thumping up the stairs, Pablo looked back to see Matias give him one last look of confusion before he turned to his left to look in the other rooms. With Ben's hands tied in front of him, Pablo hurried him to the awaiting SUV. They heard Matias cursing inside one of the hallway bathrooms.

"Fucking *mierda* did a line in the bathroom and is passed out on the floor," Matias shouted from the top of the stairs.

"Leave him, then," Pablo said, pushing Ben through the front door.

"Holding," Courtney whispered, reaching the end of the side of the house. Peeking over just enough to see around the corner, she said, "This fence runs right into the street on the left and to the right they have a wraparound driveway. I see two SUVs with the engines running. One tango is faced this way but his rifle is facing the ground. Possibly more people coming into the rear SUV's that have their doors open." There was a pause after she finished speaking as Max and the rest of the group processed what was going on.

"Max, do you see anything behind us?" Enrique asked.

"Negative, but we're sitting ducks if we stay here." He knew all it took was one grenade and their whole operation would go up in flames.

"Okay, Court, sit tight until we see who all comes out into the SUV," Enrique said. The anticipation was killing Max as he stood in the back sweating underneath all of his gear. His movements needed to be as smooth, quick and precise.

"Roger. We have movement. Three individuals coming out of the house, it's Ben in the middle. Moving," Courtney said. She rounded the corner and caught the guard by surprise, blasting him in the chest, ripping open his sternum and collapsing his body to the ground in a bloody mess. Kwame took aim and depressed his trigger, sending rounds into the back window of the SUV, trying to hit the driver. Only the sound of small cracks could be heard, the glass standing its ground.

"SUV is bulletproof!" Kwame shouted into the mic. Enrique took aim at the man behind Ben and depressed the trigger, but hit nothing. The rounds were a second too late, as Matias dove into the SUV and shut the door behind him.

Rounding the corner, Max was too late to join the gun fight. He saw no shooting and only two vehicles ripping out of the driveway. Hearing noise behind him, he turned around and caught two more guards charging them and raising their rifles. They didn't stand a chance. Max and Carlos already had their rifles leveled and mowed them down with ease, watching both bodies drop on the tiled floor.

Leaning over to Max, Enrique said, "Amigo, we have to leave now, they probably called the locals they pay as backup—" but before he could finish, the faint blaring of universal sirens could be heard in the distance. Max nodded. Just as he was about to give the signal to head back to the beach for extraction, he saw one remaining SUV parked in the back corner of the driveway and had an epiphany.

"We were briefed about an old abandoned airstrip close by they might be trying to fly out of. Do you know where it is?" Max asked.

"I know exactly where it is, amigo," Enrique said.

"What's the plan?" Kwame asked, keeping his rifle fixated on the door in case any other guards wanted to join their party. Judging by the sirens getting louder, they figured they only had minutes before being surrounded.

"Let's go get our boy back," Max said, as everyone turned to sprint to the SUV.

Fortunately for them, it was left unlocked. Max wasn't surprised; anyone who lived here probably knew who owned this house and wouldn't be caught dead trying to steal a vehicle on the property. Enrique hopped into the driver's seat and reached above the sunshades. A set of keys fell into his lap.

"Perfect," he said as throwing the key into the ignition and peeling out of the driveway into the night.

CHAPTER 15

"Alejandro, we have a problem," Pablo said. His left hand was trying its best to not slip off of the handlebar on the ceiling as their driver took wild turns down the dark roads, following the SUV in front of them. The perspiration seeping through his shirt smelled rancid and annoyed him. He wanted more than anything to get to his home in Cartagena so he could take a shower.

"*¿Qué pasó?*" came the response from his agitated boss.

"They found us, shot one of the guards, we think Santiago is dead, and we're coming earlier than expected," Pablo said, doing his best to not sound too worried. Glancing behind them, he didn't see any headlights. The only thing he had to worry about was the long pause that ensued after he had finished telling his boss what just happened.

When Alejandro finally talked, he asked, "What did they look like?"

"It was dark, *jefe*," Pablo said. "All I saw were people in tactical outfits. They could have been SEALs, *pero, no se.*"

"*Claro que sí.* Just get to the plane and text me when you land. We'll sort all this out when you get here. I have a bone to pick with our little informant." And with that, the line went dead. Pablo shoved the phone back into his pants pocket. He knew when the pretty informant picked up the phone thinking it was him, she would be in for a rude awakening.

"You can't go any faster than this?" Carlos asked.

"You try driving with the lights off using NVG's!" Enrique shouted, his right middle finger now visible to everyone in the back seat as he held it up in front of the rear-view mirror. Making the decision to keep the headlights off wasn't the worst decision Max had ever heard someone else make, but it wasn't the best. According to Enrique and Carlos, the airstrip was only twenty minutes or so away from the beach house, but after about five minutes of bouncing down dirt roads, his stomach was about to come through his throat. Putting on a seat belt was not an option because the gear was too restrictive if returning fire became necessary.

As much as Max wanted to lift his NVG's to rub his eyes, he resisted. His heart was pumping a million miles a minute and he could feel the perspiration building up underneath his gloves. There was nothing he wanted more in the world right now than a nice cold beer and a warm shower, but that was out of the question. The team was outside city limits so far that the streetlights and other cars were non-existent. All they could see through the green hue of the NVG's were trees and other shrubbery surrounding them.

Enrique took a sharp turn to the right as Max's left arm swung out and landed on Enrique's chest, trying to sustain a balance.

"Easy, *amigo*," Enrique said, "I don't think I'm ready to date outside of my race yet. I'll have to ask my parents for approval first." That got some laughs from the back row of the bouncing vehicle. After another ten minutes of climbing and dipping through the terrain, the operators spotted the airstrip sitting a mile or two away.

"Does anybody have a plan or are we just winging this?" Kwame asked, who was causing Carlos and Courtney to feel like sardines sitting in the middle, his gigantic arms pushing them against the doors. Not being able to move anything but her head, Courtney said, "First we need to get you on a diet, bro. I mean, jeez, why are you so damn big?"

"I think you need to ask yourself the question of why are you so damn small," Kwame replied.

Enrique quickly checked his rear-view and shouted, "You know what they say about guys with big feet-"

"Zip it," interrupted Courtney, "let's worry about not driving us off the cliff first and then I can hear what you have to say," interrupted Courtney, not letting the man finish his sentence. A smile formed across his face that Courtney could just barely make out through her goggles. If it wasn't for Kwame squishing her against the door, she would reach over and slap him.

"Look, there they are. Nine o'clock, down below," Max said, straining his head to get a better view of the two pairs of headlights almost to the fence surrounding the airstrip.

"Wow," Courtney exclaimed, "this place really is abandoned."

"I would go into a history lesson about it, but we have bigger issues to worry about. Max, you have any ideas about how you want to do this?" Enrique said. He had entered the downward slope phase of the road and was having an even harder time trying to keep the vehicle on the path now that it narrowed.

"I have somewhat of an idea. It's ballsy but it's the best shot we have without shooting Ben. Enrique, is this the only entrance into the airstrip?"

"Yes sir, one way in and one way out."

"Okay, here's what I'm thinking. We aim all of our concentration on the plane's wheels and hope that it doesn't take off. Roll your windows down, it's about to get really heavy really quick."

The front gate sounded like a baseball player hitting a grand slam when the front grille of the vehicle collided with it as the two SUVs pushed through. The second Pablo hung up the phone, he had called the lieutenant of the local police department and told them their situation. Pablo wanted any officers on duty to meet them at the airstrip before they got there, but the lieutenant stated Pablo and his men would reach the airstrip before he was able to put the call out. After using what remaining energy was left in his body to curse him out, he promptly reminded him who put the extra money into his pockets and hung up. The Learjet 45XR was waiting for them on the runway about three hundred yards away, and the two massive turbo jet engines could be heard cutting through the peaceful night air.

"All talk, no action," was Pablo's response. Rolling down the window to get some fresh air into the cabin, he tried to see any flashing police lights off in the distance.

"Hey, Matias, roll down your window and let me know if you see anything."

Leaning out of the window, he tried his best to look through the dense jungle, but it was damn near impossible to see anything beyond twenty yards without a flashlight, much less hear anything with the turbines screaming. "You're smoking too much of that stuff *esé*, I can't see anything," Matias said.

"Alright, let's make this quick then," Pablo said as both SUVs stopped next to the stairs leading into the plane. Matias pushed Ben out of the backseat, onto the tarmac and up the steps. Just as Pablo was about to follow one of the drivers up the steps, the hairs on the back of his neck stood up. Something was off.

The turbines were loud and obnoxious, but not loud enough to drown out the screeching of tires headed their way. Turning to the remaining driver, he said, "Go, slow them down."

The driver hopped back into the closest SUV, pulled a U-turn, and headed full speed to intercept the oncoming traffic.

"It seems we have a friend trying to greet us. What do you say we give them a nice welcome?" Enrique said.

"Everyone, get ready to let 'er rip!" Max shouted, leaning out of his window with his rifle facing the oncoming threat. Running over the gate lying on the road, Enrique pressed the pedal as far down as it would possibly go as the V-8 engine roared.

The vehicle barreling toward them stopped abruptly about one hundred yards away at the edge of the tarmac. They could barely make out the driver as he got out and ran to get something out of the trunk. The man came around the opposite side of the SUV and pointed a rocket propelled grenade launcher toward them.

"RPG!" Max shouted, gripping anything he could find inside the vehicle.

"Hang on!" Enrique responded. A loud noise pierced the night sky as a small rocket barreled toward them at full speed. Enrique forced the steering wheel to the left, narrowly avoiding imminent death. The rocket continued past them, and connected with a tree sending a large fireball and plume of smoke into the sky. Unfortunately, Enrique's sharp turn combined with the high rate of speed caused the SUV to flip onto its side. As they slid to a halt, Max barked orders. "Everyone out now!"

Enrique and Carlos were the first ones to act, grabbing whatever they could to pull themselves up and out. Enrique went toward the front and Carlos scrambled toward the back.

"Laying down suppressive fire!" Enrique screamed. Gunfire erupted, piercing the night air as Kwame was next to climb out of the vehicle, turning to help Courtney out of her seat. Max nearly flew out and was standing behind Enrique before Courtney was completely out.

"Crap, they're going to get away. We have to push!" Max said, peeking over the vehicle. The team watched the jet move forward at a decent pace down the runway.

"Reloading!" Enrique shouted, peeling back as Kwame took his spot. Grabbing Max and slamming him against the SUV, Enrique said, "No, Max! Save your energy for another day. I'm going to radio the small boats for extraction. There's a river that connects to the Gulf, but we have to get away from this airstrip."

"Dammit, we're so close!" Max screamed. Taking a second to compose himself and survey the situation, he took a deep breath and nodded at Enrique.

"Hold your fire," Max said, as the suppressing fire finally subsided. "Save your ammo until you see him."

"Okay, amigo, we're ready to roll. They'll be here soon."

"We need to cover our retreat so he doesn't shoot another rocket and blow us up in the back," Max said.

"I have that covered," Enrique said, reaching onto the front of his belt and pulling out a small green canister. "Everybody, run in the direction behind the SUV but to the fence line." He pulled the pin on the canister, took a step in front and hurled it like a baseball over the top of the vehicle.

It took a second for the canister to contact the ground, but once it did, a thick grey cloud of smoke dispersed rapidly in all directions.

"Move, now!" Max shouted. Using whatever energy the team had left, they sprinted toward the tree line. Adrenaline, flowing at full force, was pumping through their bodies, and Max was sure if there was any point in time where they could win any type of forty-yard dash, it was right now.

An explosion was heard behind them, causing Max to snap his neck back to see. Just five seconds after they had retreated, the second rocket connected with the gas tank of the overturned SUV, sending an enormous fireball into the sky and illuminating the airstrip.

The muscles in his legs screamed and ached as he picked up speed to catch up to Courtney. She was only two or three paces ahead of him; he was getting old, he thought. The fence surrounding the airport was embedded behind the tree line far enough that if anyone wanted to follow them, they would need flashlights. Even though Max couldn't see it, he heard a new threat emerging to their left off in the distance.

As the team slowed, Max shot a quick look to the crest of the hill and witnessed at least five to six flashing lights descending on the dirt road.

"Dammit, we need to get over this fence," Courtney said, breathing heavily. She shook the fence, looking for a possible weak spot. The fence was eight feet tall and had three-strained barbed wire encompassing the entire top of it.

"Move," Max said, gently shoving her out of the way. Taking off his plate carrier, he called Kwame over. "Here," he said, handing the carrier over to him. The kit felt like one million pounds in his hands and his arms and shoulders were on fire. He was completely spent. Kwame snatched it out of his hands—he knew exactly what Max wanted to do. In addition to being the biggest one in the group, Kwame was also one of the tallest. Tossing one end of the carrier over the top, it crushed the barbed wire, creating a small path to climb without getting stuck.

Kwame looked back at Max, who gave him a thumbs-up. "You first, big boy, we need you on the other side to help us get down."

"Check," he said, lifting one leg and starting his climb. The rest of the team created a small circle of protection, pointing their rifles in the direction of the SUV speeding toward the downed gate to meet the police. One by one the members of the team peeled off and climbed the fence until it was just Enrique and Max on the airstrip side of the fence.

After Max, the last one, landed on the other side, Kwame reached up and yanked at his plate carrier until it fell forward. Handing it back to Max, Kwame stepped aside and did his best to catch his breath..

"Okay, let's go," Enrique said, "the small boats aren't but a half a mile away."

"Everyone good?" Max asked. After receiving verbal confirmations from everyone, he turned back to Enrique and said, "Lead the way."

CHAPTER 16

The cellphone vibrating on the nightstand woke Alexandria from her sleep as she pushed away the stranger's arm draped across her chest. No matter how much her eyes adjusted at night, her blackout curtains made it damn near impossible to see as she fumbled to grab her phone. Sitting up, she tried her best to not disturb the snoring giant face down in his pillow.

She just went to bed an hour prior after participating in some of the worst sex of her life. This was a small price to pay for the monetary value of the information she collected for her clients. Looking at the phone, she saw a South American number and knew instantly who it was. The thought of letting the call go straight to voicemail so she could get some rest ran through her mind but answering her phone when it rang was also part of the business. If you could call it that.

"Hello?" she said in a groggy voice, trying to clear her throat.

"Miss Alexandria, do you know who this is?" said a voice she didn't recognize. Something on the back of her neck made her hairs pop to attention. Softly clearing her throat again, she responded, "No, I—"

"I am Pablo's boss," said the voice on the phone, pausing and letting the realization of who she was talking to sink in. Something deep down in her soul knew that Alejandro himself was the man on the other end of the phone. Normally, she would always ask a question of her clients and to ensure the security of the callers who she didn't recognize, but in this case she thought it was best to let it slide.

"Mr. Alvarez," she said, "how can I be of assistance?"

"I take it this line is secure? Pablo tells me this is the line he was instructed to call you on."

"That's correct, sir," she said, hoping the courtesy would help with this strange introduction.

"No need for flattering. Alejandro is fine. Now, let's cut to the chase because I would think you would want to be asleep right now, just like I would. Is that correct?"

"Yes, Alejandro," she said.

"One would think I am paying you very well?"

"Yes, Alejandro, give me a second," she said. The wooden floor creaked and moaned as she tip-toed across and opened her bedroom door. Her condo was lavish, and thanks to her side job, she could afford every bit of it. Closing the bedroom door behind her, she walked to her refrigerator and grabbed a bottle of water before apologizing, telling him to continue.

"It seems we have individuals chasing my men who know exactly where Ben is at all times. Now that leads me to believe one thing—we have a rat somewhere in my cartel that is feeding information on where my men have the kidnapped individual."

"You want me to track down whoever is undercover? I don't have access to that side of the agency."

"Miss Alexandria, do you think I am stupid, or naïve?"

"Neither."

"Good. Then let me make myself very clear," he said. Yelling was not in Alejandro's nature, so when his frustration kicked in, it was like a mother scolding her child through her teeth. "My men barely escaped a raid tonight by whatever paramilitary group was sent to rescue your friend. Although I am personally grateful at the information you have provided me so that we can be one step ahead, I need a name. I was not concerned with it before, and I didn't think we had a...*rata*...in our mists, but adding up all the events that have occurred over the last twenty-four hours or so have changed my mind.

"Now the house in Texas that was raided, I can understand because it was under surveillance by the locals, but what I can't understand is how they found our exact compound in Guaymas when it is an eight-hour drive from the border of your country. Does that make sense to you?"

There was a slight pause as thoughts were flying through her head. She had somewhat of an idea of what he was talking about, but only from what she was able to scrounge from one of the talkative members from the Bering Group at work earlier. She loved to sell secrets, but stepping outside of the agreed conditions of her contracts was not what she wanted. Could she pull up the information? Of course, although she wasn't lying about that section of the agency being on lockdown, she didn't graduate cum laude from MIT with a Master's in Computer Science because of her looks.

"You don't think the local police department had your house on surveillance in Mexico?" she asked, trying to go on the offensive.

"Unlike you Americans, we pay off our authorities, and if anyone talks, well, I'm sure you get the picture. I have resources that can find him, no problem, but that takes time and manpower. Manpower that I do not want to exercise, because it takes them away from other things that people could be doing for me. You understand?"

"Yes, I do, but that also takes away from what I am supposed to be doing, and the more I do things that aren't part of my job, the more people might ask questions," she said, getting agitated by this conversation.

"I am very aware how it works, Miss Alexandria. You will be compensated when I have my name. I need it within the next forty-eight hours."

She felt her headache increase. Climbing back into her bed was her only priority at this point, and she knew she had no other option than to comply. Even if she did say no, what would he do? Alejandro was thousands of miles away and she had followed all of the protocols to the wire. The stories were always from idiots or people who flashed their money or tried to double cross cartel members, neither of which she was trying to do.

"And if I don't?" she asked, as she took another sip of her water bottle.

"Miss Alexandria, do not play games with me. It's late and you have a three-hundred-pound behemoth to get back to, don't you?"

Her heart pounded. She thought it was going to burst through her chest. Quickly peering through her living room curtains, she saw nothing. The fear of working for a drug cartel suddenly became a reality. "Yes, I understand, Alejandro," her voice now shaking in response.

"Forty-eight hours." And with that, the line went dead.

CHAPTER 17

Enrique had promised to help the team as best he could and point them in the right direction but chasing a kidnapped American into Colombia was where he drew the line. It was approaching the early hours of the morning by the time the team arrived at Enrique's AirBnB. He let the group stay in it as long as they needed to until they could figure out where their next course of action was, but that would have to wait until the afternoon because the team was running on fumes.

Max wasn't sure how much sleep he inherited after his head hit the pillow, but he was startled awake after hearing a loud door slam. Looking at his rifle and plate carrier laying against the wall on the ground and deciding he needed something smaller to deal with this threat, he grabbed his pistol off the nightstand and jolted up, raising it to eye level. Thoughts of the previous night came rushing back to his brain and, realizing he was safe, took a deep breath and set the pistol back on the nightstand, relaxed and rubbed his eyes. The play by play from the previous night ran circles through his head as he tried his best to make sense of it all. The headache from the fatigue was catching up to him and aspirin, if there was any, would be his best friend.

Sliding out of bed, the carpeted floor feeling great in between his toes, he walked to the bathroom to take a leak. Starting the shower, cranking it to hot, he let the water fall over his skin. Ten minutes later, feeling somewhat awake, he threw some clothes on and made his way downstairs. Enrique assured Max he made no enemies when he left the Special Forces. When Max asked how it was even possible to not have enemies in a location virtually run by cartels, he just said, "Sometimes you have to get a little dirty to earn their respect." He had a feeling of what that meant but didn't want to get specific.

There were a million things going through his mind right now, but the thought of being that close to rescuing Ben laid heavy on his conscious. As much as he wanted to push full steam ahead, Max needed to be the voice of reason. The team needed someone with experience on a mission like this one.

Opening the door and looking to his left, he noticed other bedroom doors wide open. Hearing faint voices downstairs, his curiosity was piqued.

The bottom of the floor had an open layout with the stairs leading to the middle of the kitchen. The first thing Max laid his eyes on were the three figures sitting at the marble countertop. On his left was the living room with a massive television hanging on the wall displaying soccer, and in the dining room to the right was a gigantic table that looked like it could seat a substantial amount of people.

"Since when did the riffraff get sent down here to play with the big boys?" Max said, swiping his hand behind Nate's neck just close enough that Nate could feel the wind.

Nate responded without missing a beat, "We heard you needed help so we came running."

"Who needs help? Not us," Max said, yawning and leaning over on the granite countertop.

"I know a lie when I see it and that was definitely a lie," Nate responded.

"Nah, I'm glad you clowns are here. The faster we find Ben, the faster I can get back to being downrange by myself."

"What's the fun in that?" Nate asked. "I'm just giving you a hard time, man," he said, extending his hand to Max, who took it.

"Where's the rest of your goon squad?"

"They went for a run on the beach to get the lay of the land and make sure nobody is keeping a close eye on this place," he said, sliding a coffee cup toward Max. Looking to his left, he said to Kwame, "How about you big boy, you doing alright?"

"Yes, but I could barely sleep," he said, taking a sip of his coffee.

"Yeah, the bed was comfy, but getting a massive amount of sleep during crunch time like this isn't going to happen," Max said. "Who all is here anyway?"

"Everybody except Jack."

"Damn."

"We come bearing gifts," Nate said, sliding a light tan manila folder his way.

Max pushed it towards Kwame and watched him open it and sift through the documents, he continued, "We spent all day yesterday learning all we could about the Saint Bertrand Cartel and looked at every ounce of details that any law enforcement agency had on Mr. Alvarez," Nate said.

Kwame finished looking at the folder and slides it back towards Max. Not even picking it up, Max responded, "I know it's technically not early, but I just woke up. Just give me the skinny on what's inside," he said, rubbing his forehead.

"Fair enough. Alejandro Alvarez took over the cartel when he was twenty-seven, he's forty-five now and has more money than he knows what to do with. He also is very invested in sex trafficking, obviously drugs, and has several casinos in the United States. Nothing out of the ordinary, just your typical cartel member. The one thing we did find interesting though was that all of the sicarios have a small tattoo of their saint behind their left ear."

"I've never heard or seen that tattoo before. So, what do you mean he took it over?"

Holding up his hand, Nate said, "Just let me finish and hold all questions until the end, please, class." Max rolled his eyes and gestured with his hand in a sweeping motion to urge him to continue. "His uncle died from stomach cancer, and after Alejandro got back from graduating college in the states with a business degree, he decided—or more so was the last person in his bloodline, really—to take over the business. I would imagine that's why he was going to business school anyway, but what do I know. He has multiple properties scattered all throughout Colombia and various small homes throughout South America.

"We thought that most of the other small properties he owns would be for launching his product. Some, I would imagine, are reserved for vacation homes when he wants to get away from Cartagena. That's what we have on his property. When we dive into vehicles, boats, etc., he has a massive yacht that stays docked in Aruba at his beachfront home, a couple planes, and he has a plethora of different vehicles that are all registered in his name. There's a bunch of footage and pictures that we looked through and all that yesterday, but that's pretty much the meat and potatoes of it all."

Looking out the back door through the windows, Max noticed the sun's rays beating down on the water and the waves crashing onto the sand. There were a couple of people walking around and sitting on the beach way off in the distance, but no one remotely close to the back patio of the AirBnB. The aroma and the taste of the medium-roast Colombian coffee kicked in, and his five senses became more alert. He stretched and yawned one last time before downing the rest of his coffee. Just then, the back door opened as Alex, Pete, and Kyle walked through, bringing in the stench of sweat and a trail of water and sand dripping across the floor.

"I see your parents didn't teach any of you manners growing up." Max said, shaking his head and walking over to greet the remaining three members of the team. After exchanging smart-ass comments for a couple of minutes, they got back down to business and huddled around the kitchen island.

"Enrique has let us stay here for as long as we need to, to regroup and figure out what the next course of action is."

"Wait," said Alex, turning to Nate, "did you tell them about Alexandria?"

"Oh no," he said with a surprised look on his face, "I totally forgot. Good call."

Tilting his head, Max asked, "Who's that?"

Nodding his head and wiping the sweat from his forehead with his sweat-soaked shirt, Pete said, "While you guys were playing cops and robbers, some of us were busy doing actual detective work. When I went to the bathroom for a quick break, I caught a glimpse of the cyber tech supervisor. She asked me questions relating to the case like where we were headed and all sorts of stuff."

"Did you guys tell Jack?" Kwame asked.

"Yeah, he said he'd watch her and see if that's our mole."

"What do the rest of you think?" Max asked, starting with Alex.

"To be honest I don't know what to think, but if you look at all the evidence, it would make sense if there was some sort of informant feeding Alejandro or whomever information. We can start in Nogales where we had eyes on the house but they still managed to leave before we got there," Alex said.

"They could have had spotters set up around the area. I can guarantee you they had spotters set up—you don't run that type of operation without spotters to let you know when law enforcement is coming," Courtney said.

"You can't count on that," Max said. "Your spotters are called falcons in the cartel. Just more information for your future endeavors."

"Jeez, you really are a plethora of knowledge." Kyle smirked.

"Jeez, you really do like to randomly use big words to make it seem like you're smart." Max responded.

Leaning back off the island and folding his arms, Kyle didn't say another word. The rest of the group fell silent and let the soft noise of the commentators of the soccer match between Mexico and Venezuela fill the sound void. It didn't take long before Max said what was circling through everyone's mind. "Let me call Jack and figure out what the next move is. They could be any-where by now."

CHAPTER 18

When the group landed in Cartagena, Ben was once again blindfolded and taken in a convoy of SUVs to what he could only assume was Alejandro's residence. He could only guess the amount of time it took them to drive to the mansion, but for now he was more concerned with staying seated properly as the SUV bounced all over the unpaved roads throughout the countryside.

Arriving at the destination, Ben's door was opened as he was led upstairs to his room, blindfold removed and tossed inside. His survival training immediately kicked in. He walked around to look for anything he could use to his advantage as a weapon, yet there was nothing.

The room was relatively large for harboring a prisoner, and he wasn't going to complain because he knew these types of people could very well have him in a dungeon somewhere underneath the building. A small desk occupied a corner of the room along with a television hanging on the wall, and a full-sized bathroom off to the right. Realizing that this might be the equivalent of an escape attempt from Alcatraz Island, Ben gave up and threw himself on the bed. The noise from the rusty springs vibrated throughout the room as they tried their best to support his weight. If he was going to do anything, it needed to be on a good night's sleep.

The next morning, he was startled awake by his door opening. A butler walked in, holding a plate of chorizo, toast, and water, and delivered it to his desk. The trip from the night before left him mentally and physically exhausted, and all he could do was watch as the butler took one last look at him before he turned around and walked out the door. Ben watched as he continued around the corner and left his view. He left the door wide open.

Realizing this had to be a mistake of some sort, he sat in his bed for a good minute, thinking the butler would come back to close the door. But he never came. Ben's brain immediately went into overdrive, contemplating how to play the hand he was just dealt.

Why wasn't the door closed? Whoever dropped off the food had to know what they were doing—or maybe the person overheard something and was offering him a way out? There's no way, he thought. These types of people kill family members for less, which meant the door certainly wasn't open on purpose. Regardless, if he was going to make a move, it had to be now.

He snatched the breakfast off the table and shoveled everything into his mouth. When he felt the food drop into the bowels of his stomach, he reached for the ice-cold water and downed it in two gulps. Setting the empty glass back down he noticed something small folded where the glass was just sitting. Quickly picking up the paper and unfolding it, he read a three-letter word in all caps: *RUN*.

Instantly his heart picked up speed, and small beads of sweat formed on his forehead. Someone was trying to help him. Maybe there was a way out after all. Whether or not that person knew who Ben was was beside the point. He needed to escape, and he needed to do it now.

Doing a once-over of his room to make sure he didn't miss anything, he walked over to the open door, poking his head out, looking down the corridor. Not seeing anybody, he crept very quietly to the right. Not knowing the layout was going to be difficult, but what other option did he have? He could only guess someone was coming for him, but he didn't want to put all of his eggs in one basket. This wasn't the movies.

Reaching the end of the corridor, he leaned over the railing, looking at what was below. The foyer was empty, so he crept down the wooden staircase as it spiraled below.

Noticing two gargantuan double doors in front of him which he was sure led outside, he checked left and right while crouched at the bottom. He couldn't hear anything, so he tried his best to lift his legs, creeping toward the door. The wood felt cold to the touch. He pressed his ear against it, listening for clues—nothing but silence on the other end. Just as he was about to turn the door-knob, he felt a hand land on his shoulder that tossed him backward onto the ground.

In a matter of seconds, instead of breathing warm air outside, he was greeted with the barrel of an AK. Yanking him off the floor, two guards grabbed him by the armpits, turned him around and dragged him through the hallway into one of the open doors lead-ing into the dining room.

"Look who was caught trying to escape this morning," said a man sitting at the end of an elongated table which looked like it could be used in medieval times for a feast. The guards forced Ben down into one of the chairs at the other end and walked back outside, closing the door behind them. "You really thought it was going to be that easy?" Alejandro asked. "I am very disappointed that you underestimated me," he said, gesturing with his free hand for him to take the seat next to him. As Ben stood up from his chair, he walked forward and took the seat next to the drug lord. "I promise I won't bite."

There was artwork from some of the most globally well-known artists hung throughout the room. One of the more pronounced paintings was a beautiful rendition of Saint Bertrand in a white robe, sitting at the head of the table behind Alejandro, overlooking the dining room. Alejandro clapped his hands twice and a servant instantly appeared through the side door leading into the kitchen. After pouring Alejandro a fresh cup of coffee and bringing Ben a fresh cup, setting it next to him, he turned and disappeared back into the kitchen.

"You should wait a couple of minutes before you try that, I wouldn't want you to burn your mouth."

"Thanks for the heads-up," Ben said sarcastically. His first time meeting the drug lord and he pretty much fit the persona to a tee. Noticing the muscles poking out of his workout shirt, covered in dried sweat, Ben guessed that age was merely just a number to Alejandro, and that staying fit was definitely high on his priority list.

"Would you like some food?" he asked, in between bites of his toast.

"No, I'm fine, your people brought up some food to my room earlier," Ben said.

"Okay, suit yourself."

Ben reached for his cup and tried to taste the coffee, but before he could even put the cup to his lips, the steam caused him to wince. He placed it back on the table.

"Ben, do you realize how much influence I have in your America?"

"I would imagine a lot," he responded, leaning back and crossing his arms.

"That's correct," Alejandro said, finishing his last bite of toast and leaning back himself. "This is a multi-billion-dollar business, as you Americans like to call it, and I am very good at it. I run everything in this city from the government to the coffee beans that made the coffee inside of your cup. I have ears everywhere in the city and surveillance from my people all throughout the United States. Nothing moves in or out of Colombia without me knowing about it, regardless of whether it's with my people or a rival cartel. It is important that you understand that before we continue this conversation."

Ben took a second to take in everything and then nodded.

"Good," Alejandro said, "now, grab your coffee and follow me. If we're going to talk, let's talk with a view."

Ben followed suit, pushing the chairs back, as they made a soft scratching noise on the hardwood floors. Passing through the gigantic kitchen with granite countertops, white cabinets, and fancy pots and pans hanging above them all, he noticed one man, who he assumed was the chef, sitting by himself eating breakfast and flipping through a newspaper. Alejandro opened the French doors leading out onto the veranda stepping outside to admire the sun's rays coming across the valley below. The warm air coupled with the humidity reminded Ben again exactly where he was. He could see for miles around, nothing but acres and acres below, with the skyline of a city off on the horizon. Grabbing the only two chairs at the small table, Alejandro motioned for Ben to take a seat.

Sitting down, he could already feel the sweat sliding down the back of his neck. He wanted a glass of water, but he decided to just wait until the butler walked back outside.. Ben watched as Alejandro took his shirt off and drape it over the back of his chair before he took his seat. And as if on cue, the same butler who had served him his coffee had brought out two glasses of iced water, Ben was relieved.

"I want you to look around, Ben, and tell me what you see," Alejandro said. Looking out past the veranda, Ben admitted to himself, the view from where he was standing was one of the best he had ever seen. Armed guards stood almost everywhere he looked, and an Olympic-sized pool sat below with women in bikinis eating breakfast and joking among themselves.

"I see a lot," he said.

"Everything you see, I own. Do you believe me?"

"I have no reason not to," he said, drinking his coffee.

"That's correct, you have no reason not to. What is important is that you understand that people are trying to save you, but you're all alone. I'm going to make sure you're here stuck with me, perma-nently." Alejandro let that last line sink in before he continued. He needed his prisoner to know he was hopeless and had nothing to live for before he made his proposal.

Just then, the double doors swung open as two of his guards burst through, AK's dangling on their backs as they dragged and threw an haggard man who looked to be in his fifties at Alejandro's feet. Landing on all fours, the man had welts all over his face and bloodied clothes. He looked back and forth between the guards and the drug lord.

"¿*Qué pasó?*" Alejandro asked in a calm voice. Ben had to give credit where credit was due; even though he hated Alejandro's guts, he was poised in the way he carried himself, was clearly educated, and spoke nearly perfect English.

"*Jefe*, we caught him stealing." Ben didn't know what came next, but he could tell there was some sort of light arguing and of course Alejandro could understand it all, so he held up his hand, they both fell silent.

"Stealing?"

"*Sí, jefe.*"

Setting his coffee on the table and leaning forward in his chair, he had a conversation with the man in Spanish. Ben could only understand minimal Spanish and the amount he could pick up were only curse words or stupid phrases from the buddies he worked with, neither of which would help him in this instance. The calm conversation continued for the better portion of a minute after which the man was ordered to stand up. Alejandro pushed his chair back and stood with him, taking a step forward so that he was now inches from the weathered man's face.

"Ben," Alejandro said. "This man was caught stealing some of the cocoa beans from the field to sell in the market to help feed his family. What do you think I should do?"

Silence now fell over the veranda as all eyes were on him. The old man couldn't speak English, but he knew Alejandro had asked a very important question. He had no other choice but to look Ben's way. He said, "I don't know, man. He looks old so let him go and forgive him and hopefully he learns his lesson." The guards laughed at Ben's answer. Smiling, Alejandro walked behind the old man and stretched. Turning back around to face everyone and leaning on the balcony, he took a deep breath.

He put his arms on the side of the old man's head, showing grace and compassion by kissing his forehead. Walking back to his chair to face the man, he reached to his right and grabbed the pistol sitting in the pants of one of the guards, pointed it at the man, and pulled the trigger. The body slumped to the tile as blood and cranium matter sprayed all over the balcony. Ben noticed the children and the women at the pool paused to look up after hearing the gunshot, but then continued as if nothing had happened.

Alejandro shoved the pistol back into the pants of the guard, who jerked backward as the hot barrel of the .45 caliber pistol scorched his thigh. Alejandro waved his hand, and his guards grabbed the body and headed off down the steps out of sight. As if on cue, the French doors opened for a second time and two maids came out and began cleaning. Grabbing his chair, Alejandro took a seat and sipped his water as if nothing happened.

The emotions coursing through Ben's body and mind were on overdrive. Witnessing a murder like that up close and with what seemed like no remorse is what he thought he would never have to see in his lifetime. The image would be embedded vividly inside of his mind forever.

Turning to Ben, Alejandro said, "Saint Bertrand forgives, but I don't."

CHAPTER 19

Jack was sitting in the study of the office on the computer when his cell phone rang. "This had better be good," he mumbled. It was right around lunch time, and he missed his breakfast due to a meeting earlier. Reaching for his encrypted phone, he looked at the number and knew exactly who it was. "What's up, Max?"

"Just trying to figure out where the next move is," he said. Jack could clearly tell he was frustrated from the failed mission the night before.

"I have good news and bad news for you." There was a slight pause on the other line before Max told him to continue. "I just had the morning brief with Janet and gave her the rundown of what happened last night. After you gave me the GPS coordinates, the techies used some advanced math and tracked the only possible areas to land based off gas, plane size, and airports in the vicinity, and we located the plane. The flight plan wasn't anywhere in the global flight system, which was a slight snag, but we worked past it."

"What's the bad news?" Max asked, slight hesitation in his voice.

"You're not going to like this, but do you remember that mission we did chasing that idiot through Alaska?"

"How could I forget?" Max laughed. "That's the first time in my life where I thought we would have to snuggle for warmth."

"We all know you would have been the little spoon." Jack laughed.

"Don't tell me they're in Alaska because I don't feel like dealing with timberwolves again."

"No, you're not going to Alaska, you're going to Colombia.

Cartagena to be exact. Although, we can't get you too close to his mansion without drawing attention."

"I figured that much."

"We tracked the plane to just a couple of miles outside his main mansion, which is probably where he is. He feels most safe there and has most of his men and resources in the country. To be honest, that's probably where I would be," Jack said.

"I would probably be on my yacht in Aruba with the ability to sail anywhere I wanted and get away."

"That's too easy. He's very sophisticated and loyal to his country. He has half an army at his disposal on standby near his mansion, not to mention all of the personal body guards and he knows we're coming for him." Jack stood up and walked into the kitchen to get himself a beer.

"Perfect," Max said, "we're walking into a shit storm whenever we manage to get to the mansion. Let me guess, HALO jump again?"

"We can't risk it. If anything goes wrong, you'll be fucked."

"Well then lets make sure nothing goes wrong," Max said, clearing his throat.

"No, Max, if we're going to do this, we're going to do it quietly. You remember that safe house down there?"

"Yeah, of course. It's a hike, though."

"Catch a cab," Jack said in between gulps of his beer.

"I hate you, you know that," Max responded, chuckling. "And by the way, that safe house is at least two hours away."

"Then use your hot-wiring skills and snag a fresh ride. Most of them are shitty anyway so you shouldn't have an issue."

Max frowned to himself as Jack continued his speech of how this part of the mission was going to work. "When you get to the safe house, shoot me a text, load up, and await further instructions. I think I have a couple of boys deployed in the area who may

CHAPTER 19111

be able to give you a lift to Panama City. I should have more details by then," finished Jack.

"Once we get Ben, can't you have someone meet us on the coast for a water evac?"

"Negative, Alejandro has people patrolling the coast day in and day out. I would rather get you guys a for-sure exit than have to deal with that cluster fuck. There's no telling what condition our boy is going to be in when you get him, if you—"

"It'll be a 'when,' Jack, I have a feeling that's where he is," Max said. There was so much confidence in his voice that Jack wanted to believe beyond a shadow of a doubt that that's where Ben was, but he knew better. Failed rescue missions in the past haunted his thoughts when he was a part of operations of this magnitude.

"I suggest you get to it before Janet decides to pull the plug on this before you even get boots on the ground," Jack said. "And Max?"

"Yeah?"

"Bring our boy home."

"I wouldn't have it any other way, brother. I'll text you when we arrive at the safe house."

CHAPTER 20

In the early 2000's, a man by the name of Jason Reed created a private contracting security firm out of Miami, Florida. Through his years of making connections through the military and networking when he retired, Jason's business spread to new heights, quickly becoming established in other areas around the country where most of the wealthiest of clients lived. Top of the line security is what he advertised, and that's exactly why he was rated as one of the top five private companies in the United States. Jason was constantly thinking about new ways to bring in money and after the Maersk, Alabama incident. All of his prayers were answered when cargo container companies started requesting extra security.

Jason was sitting in afternoon traffic trying to navigate his way north on the 95 freeway when his touchscreen display indicated an incoming call. The caller ID said "Jack Knowles." He instantly became excited; he hadn't heard from his dear friend in a while. Pressing the green telephone button on the touchscreen and narrowly missing a purple Lamborghini who cut him off, he heard a familiar voice come to life on the other end.

"Jack! What can I do you for?" Jason asked.

Laughing, Jack responded, "Hey, man! How are you? Long time, huh?"

"I don't know what kind of special ops missions they got you running up there, but apparently it's enough to keep you busy and away from visiting old friends," said Jason.

"Oh, fuck off," Jack responded. "Don't act like you're all high and mighty yourself, Mr. CEO," Jack responded.

"You got me on that one. What's up, man?" Jason knew Jack was an extremely busy man and yet he was always willing to help him out and had done so on more than one occasion.

"Do you have any people traveling in and around the Pacific right now?"

Trying to change lanes and cursing at the new vehicle, a minivan, who just cut him off, Jason replied, "I have a team out there now actually. They're on a deployment to Ecuador and left out of Long Beach a couple of days ago."

"Perfect, how far do you think they are now from Cabo San Lucas?"

"Not too far at all. They actually had to make an emergency stop in Mexico City because one of the crew members was showing signs of an appendicitis."

Jack winced before he continued. "That sucks, I feel sorry for that guy."

"Yeah, tell me about it, but from what my guys were telling me before I left the office, they should be back underway in an hour or so. What is it you need?"

"Is the ship pulling into Panama City by chance?"

"I don't know off the top of my head, man, I have two other teams deployed to various cargo ships in the area."

"I have a team that needs assistance getting from Cabo to Panama."

"That's a big ask."

"I know, man, but you were the first person who popped into my head and if there's anyone who could make sure it happens, it's you."

Smiling and patting himself on the back imaginatively, Jason said, "Since you put it that way, I'll see what I can do."

"Perfect, thanks man."

"Don't thank me yet. When do you need this done by?"

"Tonight."

There was a long pause on the other end.

"I'll see what I can do."

"Noted, I'll be standing by. Thanks again, man."

"No problem. Oh—and Jack?"

"Yeah, brother?"

"Don't be a stranger. Come on down and enjoy some of the finer things in life. I know your old ass still likes to throw down a beer or two," said Jason enthusiastically.

Laughing, Jack replied, "Oh, believe me, when this mission is all over, I'll be begging you to let me come down."

"Deal, buddy. We'll be in touch." And with that, Jason ended the call just as the traffic cleared passed the wreckage in the right lane. Accelerating up the 95 to his house, his agenda for the evening just changed.

The sun gently fell over the horizon as Max and the rest of the team were sitting in the safe house an hour north of Enrique's house. The safe house was more of an underground bunker underneath one of the bars in the city of La Paz. The "bartenders" were newly appointed field agents who got stuck doing the dirty work before moving up to the "cool guy" stuff.

After verification codes were exchanged, the bartender Adam led them to the employee bathroom where a couple of the floorboards were loose in the "broken stall." Adam handed Max an updated note from Jack of where and how the extraction was going to occur. Covering his nose at the foul stench, Kwame helped Adam move the fake toilet, exposing a hatch and set of stairs.

Max and the team thanked Adam, who held the hatch open

while the team descended the stairs into the underground bunker. Although most safe houses were set up for extended stays, this one was designed for short durations. Once the team was inside and the loud clank of the hatch was heard above, they tried their best to get used to their new accommodations. It was outfitted like a small hotel room with a kitchen, bed, and bathroom. Luckily the odor stayed above ground as the team took different corners of the room to relax the best they could before moving again.

Hours past and when the time came, they exited the bunker through the front hatch. The foul odor smacked them in the face once more. The tunnel stretched about a mile long as Max wrapped his shemagh he always carried in his backpack, around his face. The rest of the team did the same, trying to mask the smell. Quickly making their way down the path, avoiding stepping in fecal matter and dead rodents, they arrived at the ladder, which led to an opening through a pothole in an alleyway a couple of blocks from the beach.

Reaching the top, Max pushed the ten-pound manhole cover up and to the left, quickly surveying the area. Once he saw it was all clear, the team emptied into the alleyway, closed the cover, and made their way in the dead of night to the beach. Each member took the biggest gulp of air, grateful to be out of the disgusting tunnel below.

The coordinates selected allowed for them to wait in a staggered formation behind one of the many bars closed for the night on the boardwalk looking out into the ocean. Putting on his NVG's and switching them to IR mode, Max scanned where the water connected with the sand, the team following suit. All they could do was wait and listen to the ocean gently wash up along the sandy shore as the quarter moon shined whatever light it could through the clouds.

"I think I see something," Nate whispered, tapping Max and turning his head in the direction of the rock formation to the south.

Pressing the IR strobe twice on his NVG's, Max pointed in the general vicinity of where Nate saw movement. At first Max didn't see anything, but after a few seconds he thought he saw something.

The large rock formation sat about forty yards away which is where Max saw three strobe signals flashing. Once Max received the signal, the team one by one made their way over to the formation, Max being the last one. By the time Max had joined them, one boat was already breaking the surf and headed back to the cargo ship. Crouching up to the remaining boat, a burly man in a black neoprene suit extended his hand. Max took it.

"Max Fontaine?" the man asked.

"The one and only," Max replied.

"Derrick," he said shaking his hand, "we heard you needed a lift."

Chuckling, Max responded, "A rescue is more like it."

Nodding, Max dropped his backpack and rifle in the boat and helped the rest of the team shove the craft back into the surf. Once the small boat was far enough into the ocean, Derrick informed them it was going to be at least an hour before they reached their destination.

CHAPTER 21

Alexandria checked her watch entering the front gate of the agency. She only had twenty hours left before she had to give Alejandro a call back with the results of her find. Was there a rat within the cartel? Of course. That was no different than saying the sky was blue or the grass was green. The agency had spies in all corners of the globe; it's what they did. Rolling her window down and removing the identification badge dangling from around her neck, one of the security guards asked, "Miss Alexandria, it's early for you, isn't it?"

"I suppose so, Jeff, but the early bird gets the worm, am I right?" she responded.

"Whatever floats your boat Ms. Alexandria," said Jeff, turning to his right and pressing the red button to raise the gate. She rolled her window up and continued to the parking garage located directly below her building.

After pulling her grey Audi A7 into her designated parking spot as section chief supervisor, she grabbed her Starbucks latte and headed for the elevator. Not seeing any other cars in the parking lot except for hers and one other was all she could wish for with what she was about to do. She had spent the entire day before planning and trying to figure out how she was going to get the name of the informant sneaking information while working undercover for the Saint Bertrand Cartel. Whoever it was was likely undercover for a very long time and gathered great and credible intel for the agency. She pushed those thoughts out of her mind.

After hearing the elevator's brakes come to a slow halt and the doors slide open, she stepped inside, pressed the number five and waited for the doors to close.

It was just past six o'clock in the morning. She usually didn't step foot into the building until eight. Alexandria figured if she could get the information before everyone showed up to work, that would be one less thing to worry about later. When the elevator reached her floor, she quickly made her way past the cubicle farm and over to her corner office overlooking the main road into the massive compound. Where she needed to go was on the other side, and she had to do it fast and quietly before people trickled in.

All the chief supervisors were in their own corner offices in their respective portions of the building. The main six floors were reserved for everyone except the Director and whoever worked directly with him. Wanted to speak to him? Head up to the top. Want to have a meeting? Head up to the top. She was tired of it and hoped that one day she would be able to be the one telling her subordinates to meet her at the top, but for now she had to deal with the cards she was dealt. Dropping her bag and items at her desk and guzzling down the last remnants of her latte, she tossed her coffee in the trash and hesitated before walking out the door.

CHAPTER 22

Max and the rest of his crew were out cold the second their heads touched the pillows. A nice hot shower, even if it was on a cargo ship, was a lot better than sitting in the disgusting filth the agency called a safe house back in Mexico. The seven of them were split up into four different rooms, with Courtney bunking with one of the women working for the security team. Sleeping past breakfast and realizing he was the last one to wake up in his room, Max turned the lights on and got dressed. Walking into the cafeteria and grabbing an apple to go, he left his team smoking and joking at one of the tables as he went to go look for Derrick.

Max found Derrick back in his berthing area with two other guys dressed out in gym clothes. Everyone stopped talking when he walked through the threshold.

"Max!" Derrick exclaimed with an outstretched hand and a slap on the back, "How did you sleep?"

"Pretty good actually. I didn't know you guys slept like kings on these damn ships," he said.

"Brother, these ships are over eight hundred feet long. The crew gets four-man berthing areas but since they left part of their crew at home, they gave us the two-man berthing's."

"Pretty legit right?" asked the shorter but stockier individual of Asian descent. "Larry...Larry Wang," he said.

"Max Fontaine," he responded. The other individual in the room who was an inch or so taller than Max but very skinny introduced himself as Robert. Max vaguely remembered these two from the night before, but introductions were not on their mind at the time.

Robert turned to Derrick and asked, "Do we need to leave? I know y'all have some secret squirrel stuff to talk about that us common folk probably aren't cleared for." He tapped Larry on the shoulder and tilted his head toward the door.

"You're an idiot," Derrick said, lightly punching his arm.

"Fuck it, Larry, let's go before the gym gets packed." Saying quick goodbye's, the two men left the room and shut the door behind them. Watching the door slam, Max walked over and sat on one of the beds. Derrick followed suit. Reaching over to the remote sitting on his nightstand, he made a motion for Max to lean to the left so he could hit the receiver to allow the television to come on. With a click of the button, ESPN was blaring through the sound box.

"Sorry," he said, turning down the volume, "sometimes it gets crazy in here."

"No need to apologize. Clearly I made the wrong career choice. I'm out here running around in jungles trying to not get my dick bit off by some new insect that hasn't been discovered yet, and y'all are posting security for cargo ships." Derrick laughed.

Tossing the remote back on the nightstand and scooting so his back was leaning against the wall, he said, "This business has its perks."

"How does a security firm who only protects clients get involved with cargo vessels?"

"You remember that hijacking of the cargo vessel way back in '09, I believe?" he said, crossing his arms.

"Yeah, that Special Forces team had to be called in to get the job done."

"Correct. After that whole incident, these ships took piracy very seriously, and since these companies have more than enough money than they know what to do with, they hired private security firms."

Pausing for a second before he continued, Max asked, "But I wouldn't think that there's piracy down here in the Eastern Pacific?"

"There isn't, but cartels are running rampant down here and have been for decades. When you have all this money from transporting goods and services across the globe, then I guess you say screw it. From what I was told they would rather be safe than sorry. Last thing they need is a cargo ship stumbling on a drug hand-off in the middle of the Pacific Ocean."

"When you look at it like that, I guess it makes sense," Max said. Derrick reached over for his coffee sitting next to the remote and took a sip. His veins were popping out of his arms so much that Max thought his shirt was going to explode.

"I wasn't told too much over the phone for obvious reasons, but you guys aren't here to evaluate us on our living conditions. What do you guys need?"

"What were you told, exactly?" Max asked.

Throwing his arms up to the sky to signify he has no clue, he replied, "Man, all we were told was that there was a package of seven we needed to secure on the beach. Coordinates were given to me, and I relayed them to the rest of my team. When we pull into Panama City, that's where we part ways. Now, if you can't tell me specifics, then I completely understand and I won't hound you for it. But we're not stupid. Y'all aren't some SpecOps team coming in and needing an ex-fill from a private security firm—"

"And how do you know?" Max asked with a hint of sarcasm. Derrick stopped mid gulp and gave him a hard stare before he said anything.

"No. A couple of SF dudes don't need our assistance—or do they?"

Max gave in and decided to stop messing with him. He said, "Look, I have no clue whether or not that group of people would need evacs from you guys or not, but let's just say we're in the same business, so to speak."

Raising an eyebrow before setting the coffee cup back on the desk, Derrick said, "Being honest here, a couple of guys and one gal running around Mexico with high powered guns and radios needing an evac doesn't sound like typical special operations military work. But what do I know?" Derrick said, looking at the ceiling. Max could tell he was standoffish and rightfully so. They did just rescue them from a country full of cartels, so he figured he could give way, just a bit.

"Typically we don't expose ourselves, but given the circumstances, by hooking us up with this lavish resort..."

Smiling and spreading his arms as if to say "you're welcome," Derrick let out a small laugh. "We have a buddy of ours, a teammate of ours, who was kidnapped a couple of days ago and we're trying to get him back."

Scooting to the edge of the bed, Max clearly had Derrick's undivided attention now.

"What are you guys? All I know is for my boss to call us on the sat phone and tell us to do what we did, someone very powerful has to either be friends with him or ordered him to do that."

"You could say we do the dirty work for that agency that likes to hide in the shadows."

Derrick nodded in approval. While scratching his beard, he asked, "Say no more. What else do you guys need?"

Max was relieved that he was winning him over, because the one thing he never wanted to do was come right out and tell people who he worked for. If they believed that it was the CIA or some wet-work Department of Homeland Security agency, then it was on them.

"We don't need guns or ammo, but my boss mentioned that you might be able to hook us up with a ride to where we're going."

Rubbing his thick black beard some more, Derrick thought for a second.

"While you contemplate on that, I'm going to go pee," Max said. Derrick nodded as Max walked into the restroom connected to the berthing and shut the door.

Two minutes later he emerged and found Derrick with his backpack out, a list of what looked like names, and a satellite phone. Walking to the door and opening it, he turned to Max and said, "Brother, I got you," and without hesitation or waiting for a response, stepped outside into the hallway and shut the door.

CHAPTER 23

Checking her watch, Alexandria still had enough time, provided the computer would boot up quickly. Gaining access to the corner office was a breeze using her pick and lock kit she acquired several years ago. Sitting in the swivel chair waiting for the main screen to load, she scanned the office and noticed pictures of what she could only imagine were friends and close relatives. One picture which was sitting right next to the computer consisted of a beautiful woman standing with a rifle in her hands. Alexandria closed her eyes, trying to remember what her name was, but she couldn't. It didn't help that no ones names were allowed to be on the doors.

Her name was not registering, despite the fact Alexandria was sitting in her chair, in her office. Still looking at the photo, she reminisced on her own father and the memories they shared. He never taught her how to shoot a rifle, but he also didn't hunt. Damn, she thought, putting the picture down, what was her name?

The program booted up and was good to go, so her fingers danced and glided across the keyboard. She knew the files were not going to be easy to pull up—or would they? All computers in the facility were already encrypted, so why would she have a super-secret file saved somewhere that would not be easy to access if she was the only person who was using this computer?

The first thing she realized was that her desktop was practically barren. A neat freak. Turning her head around the office, she noticed even the wastebasket was clean enough to eat in. Scrolling to the bottom left portion of the screen and pulling up the saved folders window, she noticed ten or so different folders listed, none of which stood out except for one. It wasn't labeled but it did have a lock symbol on it, signifying there was some sort of password needed to gain access into the file.

"Hmmm," she said under her breath. "This can't be too hard to crack," she mumbled to herself. She had been in the secret-stealing business for a very long time and was extremely good at cracking passwords and bypassing mainframes on computer hard drives. This trait alone was one of the reasons why she was hired right after she obtained her degree, and probably why she moved up the ranks so quickly. Her boss told her right after she made Chief Intelligence Analyst that if she kept up the great work, in a couple of years she would have his full recommendation to take his position as chief of that division when he retired. It would be at that point she would have to take a long hard look to see if she wanted to keep the business of secrets going or throw in the towel.

Five minutes later she cracked the password and a whole array of information populated. "Holy shit," she said. Well, she knew exactly where she was coming back to when she needed more information, and she knew she could charge a pretty penny for some of this stuff she was seeing. Not wanting to dive into other files and get sidetracked, she found a file named Agents.

Clicking on it revealed more subfolders listing Gangs, Mafia, Cartels, and Random. Clicking on the one labeled Cartels, brought her to an assortment of groups listed in alphabetical order. These went back for decades; some of the cartels didn't even exist anymore. Scrolling didn't take her too long as she quickly found the Saint Bertrand Cartel. Clicking the name brought up five people. Grabbing her phone from her breast pocket of her blazer, she took a picture of the names on the screen. There were no way all five undercover agents were in bed with the cartel at the same time. These were probably over the course of a couple of years.

Doing one quick sweep of the file to ensure that she didn't miss any names, she backed out of everything and shut the computer down. Getting up from the chair and making sure everything in the office was in the right place, she put her ear to the door and tried to interpret sounds outside. Opening one end of the blinds, she looked down both sections of the hallway and didn't see a soul.

Remembering to lock the door from the inside, she opened it, stepped through the threshold, and closed it as the bolt fell back into place with a small clicking noise. Breathing a huge sigh of relief, Alexandria walked back across the complex to her office. Heading back through the cubicles she felt the onset of sweat dissipating. Making it to the end of the hallway and rounding the corner to walk back to her own office, she nearly ran into the woman in the pictures.

"Hey Alexandria!" she said. "How are you?"

Surprised, she replied, "Hey! How are you? Sorry if I forgot your name, I'm still waking up. I'm normally not in this early!" she said, rubbing her eyes and giving a fake yawn.

"Oh, that's fine dear. Janet," said the woman, outstretching her hand at the same time. "You're Alexandria, right?"

Swallowing hard, and not wanting to dive too far into a conversation, she played it cool. "Yep, that's me."

"I thought so. I remember you from the all-hands conference meetings."

"Yeah, I haven't made my way to sit at the table yet. I'm still in the side chair," she said, producing a fake laugh to take her mind off the fact she wasn't supposed to be in that portion of the building.

Every Friday it was required that all chiefs and department heads met in the massive conference room on the seventh floor. People sat in ranking order from the head of the table to the end. Whoever was not authorized to sit at the table, including guests sometimes, was required to sit in one of the many chairs that wrapped around the office. Alexandria hated it but it was whatever, just new person shenanigans until someone retired or left for another job. She just wished they had more comfortable chairs to sit in.

Resting her arm on Alexandria's shoulder, Janet took a step closer, her perfume taking up the remaining space in between them.

"Don't let the men here at the big table fool you, I know when I see a strong woman. You definitely fit the bill."

Forcing a smile, she said, "I'll have to keep that in mind."

"Good," Janet replied, looking at her Omega Constellation. "Speaking of meetings, look at the time. I would invite you into my office so we could get to know each other a little but I have to run." With that, she waved goodbye, and walked around Alexandria. It was at that moment a small bead of sweat slid down Alexandria's forehead.

CHAPTER 24

Two days passed as the cargo ship made its way in the Eastern Pacific. The remaining time spent on the ship was used for planning and extensive research on the terrain the team would be traveling through. Everything was mapped out and Max made sure there were at least two or three contingency plans to every primary plan they discussed. Derrick and his team provided help as best they could, which included two Toyota Hilux's courtesy of a friend of his at the Panamanian Embassy.

After the ship had pulled in and docked successfully, Derrick and his team said their goodbyes as they walked across the brow to the waiting trucks on the pier. The rest of the ship's crew had seen the new crewmembers who magically appeared on board but knew better than to ask questions.

Approaching the truck, Max noticed a tarp in the back of both of them. "What the hell," he said, flipping up the tarp and revealing a case full of ammunition and assorted tactical supplies.

"One last parting gift," Derrick said, patting Max on the back. Max frowned knowing he didn't need the extra gear but was content nonetheless.

"Thanks, man," Max said, returning a handshake.

As Max and Alex jumped in the driver's seats, the group loaded up the rest of the vehicles, threw the tarps back over the gear and hopped in the trucks. Checking his encrypted phone now that he had service, even though it was spotty, Max saw Jack had sent coordinates in a text to a rendezvous point after they crossed the Colombian border. They were scheduled to meet with their old friend, Antonio, who would be accompanied by two small boats waiting for them. Satisfied they had a plan of attack once they made it through the Amazon, he powered down the phone and looked over at Alex.

"*Estás listo*, amigo?" Alex asked through the window of his truck.

Before Max could respond, Kyle rolled down his window. "English, bro," he said, fanning himself with his hand. "Fuck, it's hot out here."

"*Cállate blanco*," shot Alex, taking out his sunglasses from his pocket.

Kyle pulled his own sunglasses over his eyes and tilted his head back.

"How long is the drive?" Alex asked, adjusting the radio and stopping at a salsa song he recognized.

"A little over two and a half," Max said. "But if you two idiots are done, we can leave."

Smiling, pushing the shades down over his eyes, Alex held out his hand motioning for Max to take off. Shaking his head, Max pulled out of the dirt parking space, Alex following suit.

The drive from Panama City to Darien National Park where the safe house was located wound up being long, hot, and humid. Max enjoyed the Panamanian culture fluent throughout the countryside as they passed older broken buildings, children playing in the streets with withered soccer balls, and more favela's than they could count.

Once the city was in their rear view, they made it just under the time Max predicted. The two-story cabin was hidden about a mile into the dense park and off the main trail. Pulling up onto the gravel that surrounded the property on all sides, the trucks stopped and everyone got out. Grabbing the gear and ammunition crate, the team was relieved to have access to simple pleasures like simple showers and beds. Opening the door, Max saw there was nothing out of the ordinary than what someone would typically think a cabin in the forest would look like. A couple bedrooms upstairs, a living room to the left of the front door, and walking past the living room to the right, the kitchen with a small island and a small circular table. Cooking was out of the question as Max knew how far the smell and smoke could possibly travel. Risking their presence for a good steak was not on his mind.

Kwame and Alex offered to drive into the small town they passed before entering the national park and hit the small café for food. Orders were given and no sooner than they arrived, the two men were off back down the dirt path.

Max took advantage of the brief pause in operations to step outside and power up the phone to shoot Jack a text telling him everything was alright and they were going to leave shortly. He slid the phone back into his pocket and walked back to the cabin.

"Is everybody here?" Max asked, stepping into the kitchen.

"Kyle stepped outside five minutes ago to get some fresh air," Courtney said.

"Fresh air? How much fresh air does he need, he's about to get plenty of it," Max said, already getting annoyed with Kyle's smart mouth over the course of the past couple of days. Looking through the windows in the kitchen, he couldn't see Kyle anywhere. "Are you sure he went outside?"

"Yeah," Pete said sitting on the couch, propping his feet up on the coffee table. "That's what he told us, plus I heard the door slam."

Opening the back door, goosebumps ran up and down his arms. Something was off. Walking the perimeter of the cabin, he saw Kyle at the tree line toward the front of the house talking to someone on his phone.

Max took baby steps across the gravel, careful to not alert Kyle. Tilting his head to the left, he tried to hear the conversation, but he couldn't make it out. This was it, he thought, all of the smart-ass comments would come to an end and he didn't have to hear his stupid Bostonian accent anymore. Hearing him give coordinates or any type of intel gave Max more than enough authority to put a bullet in his skull. No, he thought, that's too easy for a snitch.

Getting closer to the tree line, not knowing how in the world Kyle had not turned around yet, his right hand moved away from the butt of his pistol to the handle of his Kershaw. Unstrapping the handle from the sheath on his belt, Max brought it to chest level and adjusted the blade in his hand so the serrated edge was facing forward.

Reaching the tree, Max quickly sidestepped to the right around the massive trunk and knocked the phone out of Kyle's hand with his free hand. Kyle raised both of his hands in the air as Max used his left forearm to brace against Kyle's upper chest with the blade centimeters from his trachea.

"Who the fuck was that on the phone?" Max asked, glancing at the iPhone on the ground. Stomping on it twice, he cracked the screen into a million pieces.

"My girlfriend, I swear!" Kyle said, looking like he had seen a ghost. Shaking uncontrollably, he tried to say something before Max interrupted him.

"How do I know that wasn't someone in the cartel and you're the rat that's feeding them information?"

"Bro, I swear that was her!" Kyle said, who finally stopped shaking. Max gave him a hard look up and down, and as much as he wanted to slit his throat for being a rat, his gut was telling him he wasn't it.

"Listen, you little shit," he said, stepping so close to him he could deliver a kiss. "Do you realize what you just did? These cartels have billions of dollars, you don't think they have people constantly tracking unencrypted cell phone signals deep in their territory? You don't think they won't be able to track that phone to where we're at right now?"

"Who do you think you are?" Kyle spat back. "You come here, random as fuck and expect us to listen to ever order you give?"

Max ensured the blade was pressing his skin now. Any closer and blood would be drawn. "I'm the one Jack trusts with his life to lead you through this shithole. I'm the one with years of experience, I'm the one who has established himself in this agency, and I'm the one who will be standing above your bed at night waiting to slit your throat if you come at me with some bullshit like that again."

"You're just going to kill me and think Jack won't care?"

"I will slit your throat without hesitation. Now shut up and put your hands down," Max said, placing the blade back in its home. Kyle dropped his arms. "Jack doesn't need us worrying about anything else besides getting to where we need to be. He has more than enough on his plate right now. If we get separated, you follow fucking protocol like you were taught at the FARM and I'm sure your girlfriend will hug you when you make it back. If of course Jodi hasn't given her enough hugs."

That last remark left Kyle seething with anger, but he knew better than to pick a fight with someone who wouldn't hesitate to kill him at a moment's notice. Seeing Max put the blade away calmed him down just a bit.

"There's no way they can trace that call in here, look at the thickness of these trees," he said.

"You're a true idiot you know that?" Max stepped back and took a deep breath. He waved at Kyle to follow him back to the cabin.

Stepping inside, they made their way to the living room. Kyle plopped down next to Courtney on the couch.

"So," Pete said, "you said it's roughly thirty miles, right?"

"Yep, give or take," Max said.

"This hike is definitely going to be the longest I've hiked in a very long time," Nate said, before walking to the refrigerator to grab a bottle of water. "But I can't wait to see the look on Ben's face when I tell him we had to hike thirty fucking miles and dodged rodents and insects the size of Kwame's bicep to get him." The team had a nice laugh and grabbed their gear from the living room.

When Kwame and Alex arrived at the house forty minutes later, the team scarfed down the food and sat for the next hour pounding coffee just to get one last poop out of their system. Closing the bathroom door and wafting his hand in the air, Max said, "Y'all are some savages. This is the one and only time I wish I was a woman." They had let Courtney use the restroom first. She gave a cute smile and flutter of her eyes. Max chuckled and Alex threw a wadded-up paper towel her way. They spent the next ten minutes getting their gear together and organizing and distributing the ammo and supplies from the crates that Derrick provided.

"Okay, boys and girl, it's just after one. We should reach the beach around this time early morning, possibly sooner," Max said.

"Awesome, no breaks on this train," Nate replied. "Next stop, mosquito central."

Turning to his left, Kwame said, "What kind of a lame ass line was that?" making the rest of the team laugh. Placing his plate carrier on, Nate was about to send his rebuttal when a barrage of bullets came screaming into the kitchen.

Instantly, all seven members dropped to the deck as the smell of burnt wood and gunpowder filled the room. Max and Courtney were sitting down but propped against the wall on either side of the open back door. Courtney slammed it shut with her right arm, but the sound was masked by the ricocheting of rounds around them. Looking to his right, Max witnessed the team diving for cover and trying to find the best angles for returning fire. Alex, who was lying on his stomach, was the first to shout over the gun fire.

"How the hell did they find us?" he screamed, trying to crawl to a better position over by Nate, who was already on his knees getting ready to return fire from the bottom right corner of his window.

"Nate, standby!" Max shouted as he pulled out a borescope from his backpack. This was a small handheld device controlled with one hand and had a long skinny moveable neck with a camera and light affixed to the end of it. It was typically used to look inside of barrels or small holes in the walls, but in this instance, Max nodded to Courtney and as soon as he was ready, she reached over and just barely cracked the door open. Unfolding the screen from the device, he extended the neck outside through the door frame but saw no movement in the back. Satisfied, he pulled the device back into the house and shoved into his backpack.

Courtney was now on her knees, rifle at the ready and already one step ahead of what was on Max's mind. As the gunfire ceased, Courtney asked Nate, "Do you see anything?"

"Negative," Nate said as he did a quick sweep of the tree line. Alex and Kyle were sitting by the front door waiting for it to be kicked open and exterminate anything coming through. Kwame had the left corner of the window on lockdown alongside Nate with the right. Pete had crawled his way next to Courtney during all the gunfire, the lower part of his shirt covered in blood.

"Bro, you're bleeding!" Max exclaimed, staring at Pete's gut.

Looking down at himself, he said, "Dammit, I guess I'm not Superman after all." Resting her gun against the wall, Courtney went to work as the team's EMT. Reaching into her backpack, she quickly pulled out a pair of sheers, cutting his shirt off, watching him wince.

"You'll be alright," she said, "just keep talking to me. Where does it hurt?" she asked.

"Well—" mumbled Pete, struggling to sit back up and lean on Courtney's chest.

"How's he looking?" Max asked, as the gunfire erupted again, Kwame and Nate returning fire this time. "It looks like he's going to pass out from blood loss. Stay with me, Pete!"

"Jesus, okay, we need to make moves. Do you think you can handle this while I step outside?"

"Yes, do what you have to," she said, pulling some quick clot out of the EMT kit.

"Okay, Pete," Courtney said, grabbing his head and trying to keep him conscious enough to tell him what was going to happen. His eyes were glassy and his pulse was fading fast.

"Kyle, get your ass over here now!" Max shouted. Quickly scrambling as chunks of wood were exploding all around him, he slid into Max nearly knocking him over.

"Kyle, you and I are going to head out back and push into the tree line to try to flank them from the left."

Seeing a puddle of blood on the floor and Courtney doing her best to save Pete, Kyle asked, "What happened to him?"

"He was shot. We'll worry about him in a minute," Max replied. Taking one last look at him and shaking his head, he barked one last order.

"Kwame, Nate, lay down some cover. Got it?" Max said. Alex still had his rifle glued to the front door in case the gunmen decided to be stupid and charge through it.

"Yep." They were more than ready to mow down anything that moved in front of them.

"Now!" Max exclaimed. Kyle lined up behind Max and, reaching above him to pull the door forward, both operators swiftly moved outside with their guns at the ready, scanning for targets. As the team gave cover fire, the pair made it to the tree line, fifteen yards away before they saw men returning fire back into the house. Luckily, Max only saw two of them. Not to say there couldn't be more, but he was glad it was just the two.

Kyle pushed forward another ten yards or into the rainforest to try and get a better shot while Max kept his rifle glued in the direction of the culprits shooting into the house. They were both kneeling, half-exposed behind opposite trees. Apparently, cover and concealment weren't taught to these guys.

Twenty seconds went by, and the gunfire ceased again as the two individuals stopped again to reload. How much ammo did they have? Max thought. More importantly, where did they come from? How they found them, he was *sure* he had that answer already.

"Max, I'm in position," Kyle said. "I have one, ready when you are."

"Roger, I'm golden also, engaging in three, two, one." Two volleys of three short bursts were heard and both individuals slumped to the ground instantly.

"Standby in the cabin," Max said.

"Holding," Alex said through the earpiece.

The pair moved up to the targets, each operator delivering one shot to the head of each.

"Alright, guys I want everyone ready to move in two minutes. Courtney, do what you have to and get Pete ready to move," Max shouted. Kneeling to take a better look, he noticed a tattoo behind the left ear of both dead bodies. Searching the pockets, he stopped. "Fuck," he said.

"What?" Kyle asked, scanning into the trees weapon at the ready.

Max stood up and twirled Kyle around so he was face-to-face with him yet again. "When we get back, I want your resignation letter on Jack's desk as soon as we land."

Clearly irritated at what he was hearing, Kyle replied, "That's not fair, I fucked up, sure, but you don't even know they're here because of me. How do you know they didn't follow Alex and Kwame leaving the restaurant?"

Grabbing Kyle's hand, he thrust a small tracking device, no larger than the size of a flip phone, with five LED lights on the front of the screen. "This is a cell phone tracking device. It's good within a hundred yards, so all they had to do was get a tip from one of the towers they were monitoring that you were on the phone. It doesn't take long to trace a call and when they were close enough, they used this device to hone in."

"Bullshit," Kyle said, nervous as hell.

"Walk with me." Max snatched the device back out of Kyle's hands and listened to the beeping. He didn't need to follow the device because he already knew where the signal was going to be the strongest at. His frustration with Kyle was past its tipping point. Reaching the smashed phone and kneeling, Max held the device up as it blinked and sounded so loud that he thought it was going to explode. Just then Courtney came over the earpiece.

"Max."

"You guys ready to move?" he asked, glaring at Kyle and thrusting the device back in his hand.

"He's gone," she said. "What do you want us to do with him?" Her voice lingered on the comms line. No one spoke a word. Frozen in his tracks, Kyle didn't know what to say. Max looked him square in the face with his finger pointing at his chest and spoke.

"His blood is on your hands now."

CHAPTER 25

When safe houses were compromised, it was imperative that a cleaning crew come through and get rid of any evidence placing the agency at the scene. After saying a quick prayer over Pete's body and using a bedsheet to cover it up, Max sent out an emergency text to Jack.

Pete dead. Moving.

"Let's get going," Max said, turning off the phone. The deeper they moved into the rainforest, the more humid the weather became. Moving through treacherous terrain, especially in the backyard of one of the most powerful narco-traffickers in the world, wasn't regular protocol, but it meant they were that much harder being detected. No one in their right mind would have guessed that a team would be walking through the Amazon with a GPS, hopes, and dreams that they didn't get lost.

Max knew all too well that air support and ground support was gone until they linked up with Antonio.

The last image implanted in Ben's mind on the veranda was "Saint Bertrand forgives, but I don't." He admitted to himself, he was scared.

Shortly after, Ben waited downstairs next to a handful of bodyguards as Alejandro spent time freshening up before he met them.

When he did, he said something in Spanish after which a handful of the guards jogged outside to get some vehicles.

The doors and top were off the bright yellow eighties-style Wrangler as they bounced all along a dirt trail that wasn't too far from the mansion. Taking them about thirty or so minutes, they came to a clearing that Ben recognized. There were three burnt remnants of tents and a guard tower broken in half—and here he was thinking he would never be back to this place.

"We're here," Alejandro said, motioning for Ben to step out of the car. The entourage of three other black jeeps pulled up right behind them. Ben did as he was told.

The dirt was soggy with water from the rain the night before, but he could tell by the periodic dry patches that the sun was doing its job. Looking at Alejandro's outfit—light grey slacks, brown sandals, and sunglasses—he really did push Pablo Escobar vibes. Ben understood. He wouldn't have worn a shirt either if he was in Alejandro's position, ten minutes into the car ride and he was already drenched in sweat.

Without saying a word Ben followed the drug lord to the first charred sight, then the second and stopped at the third. Turning to Ben and placing his sunglasses on top of his head, he said, "Did you know this was my favorite spot out of all of the areas?"

"I did not," Ben said. "Why is that?"

"Because this is the first place where my uncle started his operation. These tents were where the product was packaged and loaded before it was transported to the aircraft, submarine or whatever he had lined up, and you guys ruined it."

Ben could tell he was on edge, so he opted to remain silent while Alejandro contemplated what to do next. Kneeling over and grabbing a plot of charred dirt, he stood back up and dropped it at Ben's feet. "No worries," he said. "We will rebuild, and next time we'll be more prepared."

"Where do I fit in to all of this?" Ben asked, trying to develop some sort of rapport with this criminal.

"You will see in a second." Alejandro signaled for Pablo to come toward him. Alejandro pulled Pablo in close and whispered something into his ear creating a grinch-like grin creeping across his face. Walking back over to the group of ten men, Ben witnessed him yank the rifle out of one of the men's hands as he yelled at the rest of them in Spanish. In an instant the remaining nine men stripped the individual of whatever remaining weapons he had, dragged him over, and threw him at his boss's feet.

Pablo stepped in front of the man and gave him a swift kick in the face as blood shot out from his nose.

"You asked where do you fit in all of this? Do you know what this man did?" he said, pulling out a cigar and lighting it.

Shaking his head, he said, "No, Alejandro, I don't."

Alejandro took a long puff before he continued, "Of course you don't."

Without saying a word, Ben let him continue, wondering what the hell was going to happen now. He watched as the man, who was in his mid-thirties, whispered something in Spanish. Looking back at the men laughing and making a mockery of him, Ben was confused. He could only wonder what was running through his head and only kept thinking that he needed to get out of here before it was his turn on his knees in front of the boss.

"This man is an informant... or as we like to say...*la rata*. He came into my house, gained my trust and I let him lead part of my crew...*¡Mas puto!*" he said, punching him in the face. His body lurched backward as he fell, but one of the men behind pushed him forward, causing him to brace his fall. Blood spewed from his nose and mouth which quickly became embedded with tears.

Taking one long drag from his fat cigar, Alejandro pulled it out of his mouth, spat on the man, knelt and shoved the cigar into his right ear to extinguish it. The screaming was unlike anything Ben previously heard. He was now withering in a ball of pain, clutching his head as the rest of the men continued to laugh and spit on him. Turning to Ben, Alejandro pulled out a nickel-plated Colt .45 with a small picture of a saint embedded on the slide. Racking a round into the chamber, he cleared his throat.

"You asked what I want you to do? Like I said earlier, I know everything that happens. I have ears from the *favelas* to the skies and I know that a team is headed this way trying to rescue you, it's just inevitable. So, you will be one of my closest bodyguards," Alejandro said.

"And why would I do that?" Ben asked.

Waving to one of the guards, he jogged to Alejandro with a laptop in his hands. Thanking him, he told Ben and Pablo to follow him as they walked back to the hood of the yellow jeep so he could have something to set the laptop on. The rest of the men were preoccupied making fun of the man who was now lying on the ground. Flipping up the screen and typing something on the keyboard, he brought up three different live feeds, each having a small camera attached to the shirt of someone whom Ben guessed worked for Alejandro.

Clicking on the first feed, which minimized the other two, brought up the footage of someone sitting behind a steering wheel and some passenger sitting next to him. Ben couldn't tell exactly what color shirt the person with the camera had on, but he could only imagine it mirrored what his partner had: an all-white pest control long-sleeved shirt and white pants.

Pablo handed Alejandro a phone and in a couple of seconds had the people in the video on the other line. "Okay, go," he said. "Tell me if you recognize this house, Ben."

Looking closely, he watched the men getting out of the car. He recognized the cul-de-sac; it was his. He noticed his mom's Nissan

SUV parked in the driveway but didn't see his dad's car. His heart beat faster as all sorts of scenarios ran around in his mind.

"Hey man, what are you doing?" Ben asked whose face was now glued to the screen. "I get it, okay? I'll do whatever it is you want, just tell them to leave, please," he pleaded. Ben didn't know what was about to happen, but if a drug lord had people walking up to your property in gear disguised as pest control, he knew it wasn't going to be good.

"Shhh," Alejandro said, "this is the good part." The man with the camera rang the doorbell as he stepped back to stand next to his partner who was holding what Ben could only guess was a spray canister in his left hand. In his mind he was praying that for some reason his mom wouldn't open the door, although he knew deep down in his gut that wasn't an option. It felt like an eternity before the glass-paned wooden door opened and he saw his mother standing there with that familiar welcoming embrace.

"Hello," she said, "can I help y'all?"

Mom, no. Close the door.

"Yes ma'am, we're with the local pest control company and we're just offering complimentary house checks. If you wouldn't mind, we would like to look around and see if there's anything and give you an estimate? I promise we can beat out any competitors that you have heard of or are currently using."

"Lovely," she said, "that's perfect, we just had to cancel with our current company because they were beginning to get too expensive. Can I show you where they sprayed before?"

"Certainly," said the man holding the spray canister.

Every second that his mother sat talking to them and not running or calling the police made Ben want to take Pablo's pistol on his hip and shoot Alejandro in the head. The question wasn't if he could do it, standing as close as he was to him, but how many people could he shoot before he was riddled with bullets himself.

"Okay," Ben said, "I get it, now can you please leave?"

Chuckling, Alejandro looked at Pablo and shrugged. "Ben, you asked why you would want to do something like protect me. Well, this is why."

Without hesitation, Ben replied, "Yes! I will protect you, now please just tell them to go away." He watched his mother point at some of the spaces on the side of the house. She had her back to them both the entire time she was explaining. His mother opened the side gate. He watched the man with the camera pull out a pistol with a silencer from the small of his back.

"Okay, that's enough," Alejandro said into the phone. They watched as the man inserted the pistol back into the small of his back. He told Ben's mother the boss was calling and they had an emergency to attend to, but they would keep in touch. His mom thanked them as the lead man stuck his arm out to let her take them back around to the front of the property.

Raising his own pistol to Ben's forehead, Alejandro said, "I want you to listen closely so that you understand exactly what your job is, *wedo*. I have men on all three of your family members: your mother, father, and your sister. I talk to these men twice a day. If they do not receive a call from me, then they kill them, but not before they rape your mother and sister. It's quite simple. If I die, they die, and if you run, I will not chase you, but one phone call and you will no longer have family to go back to. This means that when your little rescue team comes to save you, you will do everything in your power to make sure that they do not kill or capture me."

Letting out a small sigh, Ben nodded yes as he watched the drug lord walk back over to the rat and unload his entire magazine into his body.

CHAPTER 26

A couple of hours passed as light rain fell. They created a large diamond formation as best they could: Courtney was leading the pack, Kwame and Alex were spread out on either side of the group, Nate and Kyle made up the rear, while Max took up dead center. The group remained silent for most of the hike. Heads were on a constant swivel; the team had just lost a member.

The only person who had lost someone in the field before was Max. Losing people in the field was expected, based on the jobs they were fulfilling. Max did his best to console the rest of the group, telling them it would be alright because that's what he thought they needed to hear, when in reality, it would only get worse. Coping with a death of a partner while still trying to effectively complete your task at hand was brutal, but if they weren't going to get Ben back, Max knew no one else would.

Max found it best to think about the past and meditate when trying to remove a thought from his mind when he was downrange, and luckily for him mother nature did just that. Moving through the rainforest caused him to remember hikes with his dad when he was younger. His dad always told him he was a natural at shooting, scoring in the top of whatever weapons competitions he entered since he was a kid. It translated into hunting when his dad would drag him out of bed before dawn to leave for the annual hunting trip in the Rocky Mountains. No matter what the climate was, he was always able to hit his target on the first try.

Adjusting his backpack and slinging his rifle over his shoulder, Max reached for his canteen hanging on his belt. His feet were aching but the new boots he bought about a month ago were holding up surprisingly well in this terrain. He felt no blisters yet. His shirt and pants were soaked in sweat, and although he had taken plenty of drinks from his canteen, he knew he was beyond dehydrated along with everyone else. At this point he was just praying that it didn't rain any harder because that would slow them down, and he had a timeline he wanted to keep.

Securing his canteen and stepping over a large log, he saw Courtney's arm shoot up with her hand forming a fist. This caused the diamond to halt and everyone took a knee to survey the situation. Their rifles now at the ready, everybody scanned their sectors of fire.

"Voices," Courtney said.

"Holding, everybody check in," Max said. Unanimous check-ins came across the earpieces as everyone was accounted for and holding their positions.

"I'm going to scout ahead. Alex, you want to come with?" Courtney asked.

"Roger, moving," he replied.

"Alright, make it quick, Court. If we can avoid action out here then let's do that, we don't have time to waste," Max said.

"Roger," Courtney and Alex responded in unison. Max watched his two teammates disappear into the trees. The team had no issues blending into their surroundings as their gear was camouflaged with olive green coloring, except for their rifles. Comms was nonexistent as all operators were waiting on word from their teammates as to what was going on.

"Max."

"Go ahead," he replied, removing his ball cap.

"If we keep moving forward, we're sitting on top of a ridge that overlooks a small valley, and it looks like it's a cocaine field."

"Shit," he said. "Okay, does it look like we can go around?"

"Yeah, it'll add some time, but we can definitely head to the right and go around. They won't even know we're here," Alex said.

Looking around at the rest of the group and receiving head nods from everybody, Max already knew the answer. Wiping a bead of sweat from his forehead, he said, "Roger, come back to us and we'll push to the right. I'm not trying to get into any sort of gun fight while we're in the middle of nowhere."

"Roger, pushing back," Alex responded. Five minutes later when the group had reassembled, they moved around the cocaine field.

"What did you guys see?" Kyle asked.

"There were a couple of long hut-style buildings, what looked like an outpost, a helicopter pad, and acres of cocaine plants," Courtney said.

"A helicopter pad? Damn, that is no joke," Kwame said, joining in the small talk.

"Yeah, that looks like the typical formation for the labs out here in the forests," Max said. "Obviously except for the helicopter pad. In all the labs we destroyed, I never once came across a helicopter pad."

"What do you think that means?" Courtney asked, taking a swig from her canteen.

"Who knows, probably a major production site. How many guards did it look like were down there?"

"At least ten that I counted," Alex said.

"There's nothing that we can do now but keep moving. It's a shame you guys weren't there to enjoy the old operations Jack and I used to get into down here," Max mentioned, ducking to avoid a low-hanging tree limb.

"We have a long hike. I'm sure we would all be intrigued as to what you're referring to," Nate said, glancing over at him with a smirk.

"Negative my friend," Max said, "classified operations, playboy."

"We're literally in the middle of this forest. Who's going to hear us?" Kyle asked.

Max shot him a look and didn't have to say anything. Kyle took the hint.

"Those were simpler times, guys," Max said, "we could get away with so much more back then."

CHAPTER 27

Jack's phone was sitting on the nightstand when it vibrated, waking him from his sleep. He had only been home a couple of hours before he fell onto his bed, fatigued from meetings all day. Who could possibly be calling him this late at night? The caller ID said Janet—Oh, Lord, he thought. He reached for the remote, pressed the mute button on the television, and answered his phone.

"Yeah," he managed to mumble, rubbing his eyes.

"What are you doing?" Janet asked.

"Oh, I don't know, I was contemplating going for a swim. I hear the ocean is great this time of night." He hoped the sarcasm would squash any useless banter she was trying to bring to the phone call.

"Well, let me in, I'm right outside."

"What?" Jack asked, now getting out of bed to look outside his second story window. Sure enough, sliding the curtain back just a tad, he saw her E-class Mercedes-Benz parked in his driveway, as she was waving something at him.

"Look, I know it's late, but we need to talk. I have a bottle of bourbon with me."

The thought of grabbing the Springfield .45 pistol that was sitting on his nightstand and accidentally shooting her and saying she was an intruder ran through his mind.

"Hold on, I'll be right down." He grabbed a robe from the closet and threw on a shirt and gym shorts. He made his way down the spiral staircase leading into the entryway. His house was covered with random pieces of artwork from all over the world and different time periods. There was a big red carpet that sat on top of the wood floors of the entryway which he didn't particularly like, but his late wife had bought when they moved in twenty years ago. He switched on the porch light and the entryway chandelier and opened the door.

Janet was wearing a short-sleeved shirt, sweatpants, and sneakers, clutching her whiskey bottle as promised. Stepping inside of Jack's house, she took a second to admire the paintings and chandelier as he closed the door behind her.

"Make yourself at home," Jack said, clearly still exhausted. Looking at the bottle that was half empty, he said, "I see you started without me?"

"No," she said taking off her shoes and putting them by the door. "I don't drink, but my boyfriend does."

A blank expression came across Jack's face, "Since when do you have a boyfriend?"

She replied, "I do have a life outside of the agency."

"Fair enough," he said, waving for her to follow him through the hallway and into the kitchen. She looked at all the pictures of him and his wife hanging throughout the hallway but knew not to mention anything. She had died two years prior, losing her battle with breast cancer.

"You were sleeping, I take it?" she asked, pulling out the barstool and taking a seat, setting her keys on the counter.

"Yes, I was."

There was a brief silence as Jack opened the brown cabinet to grab two glasses and some ice from the freezer before he set them down on the granite countertop.

"What's so important that it couldn't wait until morning?" he asked.

"Before we go there, I need to get something off my chest," she said, pouring bourbon into both glasses. "I want us to be on a fresh start."

"Well, maybe I should be in charge of the Bering Group and not you," he said, his exhaustion clearly letting his 'I don't care' mentality get the better of him. Letting the burning sensation linger in his mouth after taking a swig, he was impressed.

Taking a sip of her own before she continued, she said, "I get it. And you can still hate me all you want to, but we still have to work together and I don't think that us always arguing in front of the children is a good thing."

"In front of the children? You mean the grown adults that you never check on to see how they're doing when there's no mission involved?" Jack asked, more direct than what he wanted to be.

"I do think people are noticing."

Jack stared at her for a couple of seconds before he looked down into his glass. Leaning on the countertop across from her, he rubbed his eyes again as he caught a glimpse of the time above the microwave. It was just past ten-thirty at night. Giving a loud and obvious sigh, he swirled the liquid in his glass.

"I hear nothing but good things about you from literally everybody. I am past the age of trying to smooth over anyone who I genuinely do not like, and you unfortunately fall into that category."

"Why do you hate me so much?" she asked, setting her glass on the counter.

"The Bering Group is my baby and I want to see them through until I leave the agency. I want to be the only person that's involved with them. I want to be the one to report to David for of their findings, I want to be the one that is responsible for everything that there is to do with the group. I guess when David told me that I had to report to you, I was a little jealous—"

"—a little?" Janet laughed. "If I remember correctly, you wanted to snap my neck in half last time we met."

Letting out another sigh before he took another sip of the brown liquid, he said, "I know, and I don't apologize for it. But you're going to have to get used to my personality if we're going to be working together. I've been here for too long to just up and change the way I feel about you at the drop of a hat. If you want to win me over, you're going to have to prove yourself to me, and waking me up this late at night doesn't help."

"Even with a bottle of bourbon?" she said.

"It's a start, but only because it's a good bottle."

"Jefferson. It's all I drink." She said, raising her glass as they both downed the remaining liquid. Grabbing the bottle and pouring a second round of drinks, she continued. "We have a little bit of a problem."

"I still have to arrange the small boats to be at the rendezvous point for the team tomorrow?"

Janet stopped mid-pour as a serious expression swept across her face. "You haven't done that yet?"

Jack smiled this time. "I'm kidding."

Capping the bottle Janet said, "Not very amusing. But I think we may have someone trying to gain access to the server."

This stopped Jack in the middle of his next drink. Setting his glass back on the counter, he leaned in closer to her as if they were in a crowded bar and someone was sitting behind them. "Keep going."

"This morning when I got to my office, everything was fine. The door was locked before I opened it, the room wasn't in disarray, and none of the files on the computer were missing—"

"Then what's the problem?"

"How much do you know about me?"

"Other than you're close to your dad and you like to go shooting, not much else."

Taking a sip from her glass, she said, "I take it you haven't been to my office, correct? Like ever?"

"No."

"Well, if you had, you would see that I am a bit of a neat freak," Jack didn't seem disturbed in the slightest but let her continue. "I think it's two-fold. I think because of the position that I'm in, I would like to think that I take extra precautions around my work and private life to ensure that it doesn't get compromised."

"Continue," he said, leaning back and taking a sip.

"I don't have fancy cameras in my office like some people do that record things at all times of the day, but I do have a very unique security system."

Janet saw Jack's eyebrows raise as if a question was brewing in his brain. "My dad was in the military for over twenty-five years. He was a Marine. They taught him lots of valuable principles, etc., that he's passed on down to me and my brothers. Some were shooting, some were hunting, how to track through the woods, etc. As important as all of those were, do you know what the one thing he valued the most was?"

Taking another sip from his glass and setting it down on the counter, he didn't care. Jack's mind was so crowded with a million other things than to be bogged down by whatever story Janet was telling. His eyes were growing extremely heavy as drowsiness swept over his body like an angry force beckoning for an answer.

"It was security. Security was his biggest principal that he wanted to teach us, because nothing I said before would matter if we didn't take care of ourselves and our family. Now—"

"Jesus Christ, Janet, I love the story but can you get to the point?" Jack said, wanting more than ever to crawl back into his bed upstairs.

Giving a blank stare, she continued. "What I'm saying is that I had a picture on my desk to the right of my computer. It was a picture of my dad and me on a hunting trip. Since electronics—I don't care how advanced they are—can be erased and deleted, I decided to develop my own security system for my office. I dust everywhere in my office once every two weeks, except that partic-ular picture on my desk."

"Interesting security system, but I kind of like it."

Looking down into the rest of his glass, he thought a moment before raising it to his mouth. He cocked his head backward and finished the rest. Setting it back down on the counter, he looked at Janet as she held hers in her hand and was letting him ponder on the information just passed to him. She knew he was tired and ready to go to bed so she followed suit and gave the empty glass with a little bit of ice left, back to Jack.

"Were you able to get the prints somehow? You realize that this is a pretty big deal, right?" Jack said, rinsing out the glasses.

"Of course, Jack, and yes to both," she responded, reaching into her purse and pulling out a small baggy with a piece of tape inside. Examining the contents, Jack felt satisfied and set it on the counter.

"Why didn't you just go to David with this? Why did you come to the person who works directly below you and not above?" he said, leaving the glasses in the sink and leaning on the counter now to look at her and crossing his arms.

"Honestly, I figured I could come over and try to smooth things over with you. Judging by the way this conversation is going, I would imagine it worked?"

"It's a start."

"Look, you and I both know that if I go tell David, as good as a friend he is to you, he may or may not blow this way out of proportion."

"No, what's probably going to happen is if you tell him some person came in and ruffled some dust around your desk and you got their fingerprints, he's going to look at you like you're crazy and probably start to rethink you taking over his position when he retires. He won't believe someone was able to get into your office or hack anything for that matter."

Getting up from the barstool, she grabbed her purse and stretched a little. "Can you figure out whose prints those are without causing a storm?"

"You should have brought me something harder to do with my spare time."

Jack followed her through the hallway and watched as her perfect figure knelt over to put her shoes on. Looking at her, he asked, "Do you know who it is?"

Opening the door, she said, "I think it's Alexandria, but I can handle the team. I just need you to figure this out before it gets out of hand. Your sole job now is to get these prints processed." She handed Jack a small plastic bag with some fingerprints on a piece of tape sitting on the inside.

"Fine, goodnight."

Thinking it over, he realized he wanted nothing more than to be with his team, but if secrets were going to be exposed about the agency, then he had a duty to stop them. That went above and beyond his team. He held the door open just a little longer as he watched Janet disappear into the darkness.

CHAPTER 28

The sun's warm rays poked through the treetops and onto the team moving below. A long night with no sleep plagued them, but they knew stopping wasn't on the agenda. It was just after noon by the time they reached their rendezvous point but before the team ran out into the open, even though they were certain that nobody was watching them, Courtney pulled out a compact drone and within two minutes had it flying.

None of the other members besides Ben took any interest in anything other than shooting guns except for Courtney. She had always said, "You can't always shoot yourself out of a situation." This was one of those times. The four rotors allowed the drone to hover upwards of two miles and also aided the drone in being quick and nimble, the perfect match for the required task at hand. As the six members guarded Courtney with their rifles at the ready, she engaged the thermal imaging button, allowing everything on the screen to turn different hues of red and orange. After confirming with Max the various heated signatures about half a mile away, and closing on their position from the other side of the river, she landed the drone and packed it away.

"Are we certain that's them?" She asked.

"Positive, but stay frosty, folks." Max responded.

Nicknamed *Hombres de la Muerte,* or Men of Death, Antonio and his men were known all around Cartagena as the elite tactical operations group nobody seemed to mess with. While Colombia had its own special operations military groups that trained and did their own set of missions, the Men of Death did more local operations involving taking down people in drug trafficking, harassing police officers, and grabbing criminals who were on the run across the country.

The Men of Death fell under the National Police of Colombia, which in turn was controlled by the Minister of Defense. This allowed them to operate wherever they deemed fit to deal with lower-level crimes so that the Special Forces didn't have to get involved. The name, however, came just a few years prior when the Saint Bertrand Cartel was running rampant all throughout the state. Instead of capturing the sicarios and lower-level men to bring them to justice, the Men of Death would simply find members of the cartel and kill them on sight. They never exposed themselves and always wore skull masks during operations. The cartel had no clue know who they were. Sure, there were leaks and dirty police, but the police officers who knew them knew better than to give them up because if they did, Antonio and his men would find them and make sure they didn't talk again.

Squinting to the west, Max thought he saw something shiny on the other side of the river. After leaning forward and reaching for his binoculars, he brought them to his eyes and focused on the area where the light was coming from.

"Did y'all see that?" Max asked.

"See what?" Kwame said, now trying to see where Max was looking.

"I got 'em," he said, pulling out his small flashlight and clicking the light in three quick successions. The two-thousand lumen flashlight broke through the dense trees and brush as a response light came just as quickly from the other side.

"Okay, folks, let's go," Max said, standing up and moving forward toward the opening.

Looking confused, but trusting Max, the team calmly followed him out into the open. Once they saw ten Hispanic men dressed in camouflage fatigues and skull masks, they instantly felt at ease.

The river was around one-hundred yards across and not nearly shallow enough to walk through without sinking to their chest. Slinging his rifle across his back, Max brought his arms up to his mouth and used his hands to cover the sides of them to help project his voice.

"Just like old times!"

"Amigo!" came the response from the only operator standing on the other side of the river, pulling his mask up. The rest of his men formed a perimeter with their weapons drawn except one who was talking on what appeared to be a satellite phone.

"Why isn't our limousine here yet, brother?" Max asked, laughing.

"There's no limo's down here my friend. All that fancy stuff is on your side of the border," responded Antonio.

The rest of the teams energy was drained. Everyone, except for Max, who was busy trying to get a signal on the satellite phone himself, was perfectly content with falling asleep where they sat but knew they had to keep going. The devastating sun coupled with the humidity and sweat had caused all their bodies to be extremely dehydrated.

Putting the phone back in the pack and downing the remaining water in his canteen, Max perked his head up. Hearing a soft hum of some sort of watercraft, the rest of the team stood up and instantly took defensive positions around the log and large boulders surrounding them.

"Relax my friends, that's our ride!" Shouted Antonio, raising his arm and forming small circular motions in the air indicating to his group that it was time to leave.

No sooner had he said that than two thirty-foot dark grey tactical speed boats ripped around the corner, causing a large swallowtail behind them. The boats slowed down to a mild two or three knots and Antonio instructed Max and his crew to be picked up first.

The boat pulled up as close to the sand as possible without completely beaching. Two mounted machine guns occupied the port and starboard sides of each boat along with small shields that surrounded the sides of each barrel to protect the shooter using the mounted weapon. The coxswain slowed down allowing both men in black tactical gear to hop off their mounts and help the bodies on the beach into the boat. While this was going on, the secondary boat stayed vigilant, manning their guns and sweeping the beaches for any random assaults. Max's team did their best to not spend too much time in the murky water for fear of what lurked beneath the surface. Once everyone was on board, the process repeated for Antonio and his crew.

The coxswain leaned away from his joystick and directed the team to sit on the deck. "Sorry, everybody," he said in English. "We had to strip the seats to make these things lighter. The river here isn't that deep despite how wide it is. Also, be ready for a bumpy ride when we reach the ocean."

"How long is the ride?" Courtney asked, who had to yell to talk over the engines.

"A little over an hour." Satisfied, she sat back down next to Nate, who was completely sprawled out, lying on his back. Looking over at her, he said, "I could go to sleep right now."

"You're not lying," she said, laying her rifle down and facing the other direction. All sorts of emotions were flooding through Max's head: exhaustion, sadness, rage, and fear. He was a professional and he knew more than anyone else that now was not the time to let emotions get the better of him. Especially when they were in the home stretch. Frustrated the satellite phone call didn't work and he couldn't contact Jack, he took a couple of deep breaths to try and relax.

CHAPTER 29

It took just over an hour in total for both boats to dock, unload the passengers, and for Antonio and his crew to drive everyone back to Monteria, Colombia. There were two large blacked-out armored van all sixteen members crammed into that surprisingly had space to fit four more between both vans if needed. The operators driving the boat stayed behind to trailer them and would meet them back in the city. Once inside, Antonio put his hand up to his mouth and signaled for them to stay silent for the duration of the trip.

Making a left into what Max assumed was the police station, he could barely make out a big rusted iron gate propped open and leading them over a gravel parking lot with a couple of squad cars parked in front of a pair of steel double doors. A couple of policemen could be seen talking to each other that didn't seem to care about the two large blacked out vans that drove past them. It must be an everyday occurrence down here, Max thought.

Driving to the left of the police station, the van slowed down and made a right to drive around to the back of the building. Parking backward and making its final stop, the driver and passenger hopped out of their seats and opened the back door where the hot humid air instantly hit the team in the face and reminded them just how far South they were.

"Put your baklavas on," Antonio said to his new American friends, who were the last people to exit the back of the van. Following his instructions, they walked behind him into a second building not attached to the main police station. Antonio's men held the door open as they watched Antonio type in an access code, then the team followed them through the tinted glass doors.

The only thing inside the room was a door to the left and an elevator in front of them. Walking to the elevator, they saw that there was no button, only a small glass screen. Antonio walked up, took the glove off his right hand and pressed his thumb up against the panel. Once it scanned his heat signature, the elevator doors opened, and the entire team stepped inside. The doors closed behind them and then the elevator lowered them into the ground.

After a couple of seconds the elevator stopped moving and the crew stepped out of the elevator. As people began filing out of the elevator, Max and the team stayed back watching Antonio's men make their way through the cubicle farm and into the locker room. Once the doors closed, Antonio finally took his mask off and instructed everyone else to do the same, and then he spread both arms as wide as he could to embrace his old friend.

"Max, *amigo, ¿que paso?*" he said.

Max responded, "The usual."

Taking a step back from embracing his old friend, Antonio turned to the rest of the team. "I apologize for the late greeting, but welcome to Colombia," he said, now shaking their hands and introducing himself.

"When did it get this bad where we can't even talk in the back of your van?" Max asked.

"It's gotten really bad here, my friend. We've had the van bugged a couple of times and we think it was some dirty cops trying to get some intel for the cartel. Ever since then, we don't say a word," Antonio said, patting Max on the shoulder.

Turning, Antonio led them through the small, mostly empty cubicle farm. Leading them to a small closet sitting between the men's and women's locker rooms, he opened the door to expose an entire closet full of towels, soap, and whatever other toiletries would be needed for an overnight stay. He also instructed them to each pick a locker inside and assured them that their gear and weapons would be safe.

"Damn, man," Alex said, "this is a pretty legit set up, who has the offices and other doors on the sides of this floor?" He pointed to the edges of both sides of the cubicle farm at a couple of closed doors leading into private offices. One door marked Conference Room and another door marked Cafeteria were wide open. Squinting into the cafeteria, Kwame said, "I will definitely be in there after this shower."

Laughing, Antonio responded, "My friend, all of you, any friend of Max's is a friend of mine. Help yourselves to whatever you need in this closet and afterwards have as much food as you like. Anything you see in there is fair game. You have cots set up in the spare duty room in the back of the building which I'll show you all to later. Max, lend me your ear for a bit if you don't mind."

"Yeah, of course," he said, turning to leave with his friend.

"Don't eat all the food before I get in there, Kwame," Kyle said, who received a quick scolding from Courtney. Once the team dispersed into their respective locker rooms, Max followed Antonio into the Conference room. Following his old friend, he took off all his gear and weapons and laid them by the door. An intense wave of euphoria swept through his entire body when he placed the last piece of equipment, his Dodgers ball cap, onto the desk. Falling into the comfortable chair, he knew he would only be able to sustain a little bit of conversation before the wave of drowsiness led him to fall asleep. Thinking to himself there would be plenty of time to sleep after they rescued Ben, he forced himself to stay awake just a little bit longer.

Antonio picked up the remote and turned off the soccer match playing on the sixty-inch television screen hanging on the opposite side of the room. After taking a deep breath, Max turned to Antonio. "What's up?" he asked.

"It's gotten pretty bad around here the last couple of years. We've found wires inside our squad cars tracing them back to the Bertrand Cartel, and a couple of police were found to be informants for them. The level of corruptness in politics that has transcended this great country is unmatched to anything that I have seen in my years of living."

Crossing his arms, Max responded, "Somehow, I am not surprised."

Chuckling a little bit, Antonio responded, "I guess to you guys on the other side of the border, everything appears like all the countries to the south are corrupt, but I promise you it has gotten worse. My men can be trusted, I can guarantee you that, it's our sister building next door."

"Is that why you guys have everything underground?" Max asked.

"Not really, before this was even an area, we were all stuck in that building. We were all crammed into one of the corners on the second deck, while this bottom portion we're now sitting in was only the cafeteria and the conference room. So, after sweet-talking the Captain, I convinced him to let the Special Operations Division move down here to free up space and to hire more people on the force when cops upstairs were popping up left and right as informants to the cartel."

"Smooth move. I like the new digs," Max said.

"It's definitely better than being cramped up there."

"Where did y'all get the funds to pay for the high-tech gear? And don't think I didn't notice those speed boats out there either," Max said smiling.

Leaning back himself, Antonio said, "That's what happens when you confiscate truckloads of money and the corrupt politicians don't want to put it all in the media. It gets lost and doesn't even go into evidence. Our Captain, who is very much against any form of cartels in this country, said eff it. So we started using their drug money to build up our police force."

"Sounds like a smart man."

"Oh, he is, but let's not talk shop, or at least not mine. I talked to a woman named Janet this morning and she said for you to give her a call."

"Yep," Max said. "The sat phone wouldn't work in your stupid rainforest."

"Go ahead and use my office. When you leave this room make a left, and it's the first door on the left. Your phone won't work down here, so just dial star four five and type in whatever number you need to. And don't worry, all phone lines down here are encrypted, so nobody will be listening no matter how hard they try," Antonio said.

Giving him a thumbs-up, Max slid his chair back and walked out of the conference room. The conversation lasted all of five minutes before Max was back in the conference room. Sitting back in the same chair, he found Antonio had brought him a bottle of water and he was drinking out of his own.

Twisting the top off, he said, "Janet is Jack's boss, and she thinks we have a mole in the agency. We thought so before, but just weren't sure."

The dark brown eyes of the tired Hispanic man widened at hearing the news. "Who does she think it is?"

"She won't tell me, but apparently the crew thinks it's this attractive blonde who works on the fourth floor—none of that matters; she'll be dealt with swiftly if that's the case. Jacks looking into it."

"Damn, I guess it's not just this country that is corrupt then, is it, my friend?"

"Not a word to anyone else about this. She said she was very hesitant to even tell me, but she said my skills might be needed when I get back."

Taking another swig from his bottle, he said, "What does that even mean?"

"It means someone may or may not make it to see her birthday when I get back, if you catch my drift."

"Sounds like fun," Antonio said.

"It wont be for who I have to take out, I can promise you that." Max continued. "Janet also said, as far as location, they think our guy is in Alejandro's mansion. Which, once again, we figured that but we just needed a definitive answer. They have constant surveillance over it and have phone calls talking about a new person in one of the bedrooms. How long do you think it'll take us to get to Cartagena?" Just then, Courtney, Kyle and some of Antonio's men trickled into the conference room.

"Slow down, buddy, you can't just waltz into Cartagena and roll up to Alejandro's mansion without him noticing you're coming. His mansion is on top of a hill thirty minutes outside of the city, and it sits below a big cliff. He's very smart. It also sits on ten acres of land and there's only one road leading in and out of his property. On top of that, the second you make the left onto it from the main highway, he'll know we're coming. He has lookouts everywhere in the city, intense security around his home, the army base on standby close by, and not to mention random guards scattered all along the road in the forest that surrounds it on both sides until you reach the clearing at the top."

"How do you know all of this?"

"We've raided his property a couple of times and every time he gets the charges dropped. It's to the point we stopped conducting them until we've compiled enough evidence—"

"But the evidence won't sustain anywhere in court with the judges that I'm sure are on his payroll?" Max interrupted.

"Yes," said someone else, taking the seat next to him. "Ricky," the man said, extending his hand. "Max," he responded, holding out his hand and doing the same. Ricky's demeanor suggested he saw plenty of action and had definitely been around the block. He never made eye contact and just kept his eyes glued to the rice and eggs that were in his bowl. It was amazing to Max how much life was sucked out of people when dealing with this type of threat.

"All of the men who helped me today would give their lives for one another. They've been briefed on the operation and are more than willing to go forward and rescue your friend. However, I have a favor to ask of you."

"And what's that?" Max asked, raising his eyebrow and crossing his arms.

"We will rescue your friend, but you will help us kill Alejandro. He's had a strong hold on this country for too long and has too many people in his pockets. Everybody fears him and his sicarios. They're like the Egyptian plague, the locusts eating up everything in their path, leaving nothing behind. With him dead, his organization will crumble, and we can finally finish what we started long ago," he said.

"Fair enough," Max replied.

"Good, now go take a shower," Antonio stated, "you stink."

CHAPTER 30

Jack's knew in his gut already who the mole was, but he needed to make sure. Pulling up to the security office, he walked up to the doors and stepped inside as younger people dressed in casual business attire walked by him. Entering the building, the smell of fresh bleach from the clean floors instantly stung his nostrils.

To the right and left were nothing but rows of empty seats with TVs hanging on either walls. One was broadcasting Fox News and the other ESPN. Nice to see nothing has changed, he thought to himself. He walked up to the bulletproof glass and asked the young woman where her supervisor, Jeff, was. Looking up from her tabloid magazine as if he were annoying her with such a mundane question, she hollered for Jeff. He thanked her, and she shook her head and went back to her magazine.

Jack stepped away, paying attention to the television screen where two commentators were arguing with one another about police brutality and the upcoming election.

"Jack!" He heard a familiar voice from behind him. "*The* Jack Knowles! How are you?"

Turning around and embracing his old friend with a partial handshake and hug, he answered, "Really good, man! How's the job treating you?"

"Great, Shelly is finally graduating high school and Sean is doing pretty well at Dartmouth. Although I had to tell him once or twice to not let the girls distract him from his grades." Both men laughed. "What can I do for you, man? It's been a while since I've seen you."

"I know, and I've been trying to have you guys over for dinner, but I've been swamped lately with work. That's why I'm here, you got a moment to talk?"

Nodding, Jeff said, "Here, follow me into my office." Jack followed him through a side door and down a small hallway. Entering his office, he noticed pictures hanging on the walls along with previous accolades from his time in the Secret Service.

The two had met one day when Jack's battery in his car was dead on the facility. Making his rounds around the massive base, Jeff pulled over and let Jack borrow a pair of jumper cables. They made small talk as his car battery was charging. Once they found out they grew up in the same city—Austin, Texas—it was a match made in heaven.

Taking a seat in the leather chair across from the massive glass and mahogany desk, Jeff leaned back and kicked his feet up on the desk.

"You think you're someone important now or what?"

Jeff responded, "I don't think I'm important, just more important than you."

"Go fuck yourself," laughed Jack, pushing his feet off the desk.

"Enough small talk, have you heard anything about what's going on?" Jack asked, anxiously.

Jeff said, "Only that someone from the agency," gesturing to the massive complex on the other side of the building, "was kidnapped or something, nothing more. And you already know I'm the only person who ever hears anything down in this office. I may not be an agent, but seniority has its perks around here," he said. "And don't worry, if I hear anything of interest I'll give you a shout."

"Good, so, that's kind of the reason why I'm here. I need a favor."

"Yeah, name it."

"Can you show me the cameras for the last twenty-four hours?"

"Lock the door," he said, turning to his computer and banging away at the keyboard. In the amount of time that it took Jack to stand up, walk to the door, and sit back down Jeff already had the video camera files pulled up on his computer. Turning the monitor so that both men could see the same screen, Jack witnessed four video files on display.

"Okay, so what am I looking at?" Jack asked.

Pointing to the first screen in the top left corner, "All of our files are organized by fours inside of their respective locations wherever the cameras are that we are trying to access. There being twenty-four hours in a day, each video is broken up into six-hour increments and after a full seven days, they are all transferred to a massive storage unit that is actually located in the main compound."

"I know about the security compound in the main building, but I didn't know all the files got shifted there," Jack responded.

"Yeah, I started that about a year ago. We can access any and all security files, but I figured that the safest place for them is inside on of the safest places in the country. That way no one can come in this building and just erase the files."

"I'll give you that. You do realize that by you saying that it is one of the safest places in the country that you're touting your own security detail and that's a pretty big bullshit claim," Jack said, trying to get a rise out of his old friend.

Leaning back from his chair and staring at him, Jeff said, "Do you want to take this outside, old man?"

Chuckling, Jack responded, "Relax, I wouldn't want you to break a hip."

"Who are we kidding? We'll both probably break something if we start to roll around in the grass."

"You're also seven years younger than I am," Jeff said. Getting back to what they were looking at on the monitor, he said, "Where exactly do you want me to pull up?"

"Let's start with the front gate at around five o'clock yesterday morning."

Jack watched Jeff click on the file, which opened another file with labels just like he said of locations on the complex. He moved the mouse over the one labeled "front gate." Clicking on it opened a video which he expanded taking up the entire screen. With the enhancements in technology, everything looked super clear and crisp. Clicking play, Jeff leaned back but kept his hand on the mouse indicating when Jack wanted him to stop.

"Keep going until you hit eight o'clock," Jack said, who was now so close to Jeff he could smell the ham and cheese sandwich he had for lunch.

"Do you have any gum?" Asked Jack, crinkling his face and leaning back for a second to get some fresh air.

"Yeah, why? You want a piece?" Jeff said, reaching into his drawer and pulling out a stick of gum. Handing it to Jack, he refused to take it.

"That's for you, not me bro," Jack said, watching his friend pause and raise his hand to smell his own breath. Nodding silently in agreement, he peeled the gum foil back, popped the stick in his mouth and continued with the computer files.

"Thank you," Jack said.

"Jeez, you went soft." Stealing a glance at his old friend, Jack did nothing but raise his eyebrow. Jeff smirked and continued, "Jack, there's so many cars, if you tell me which one you're look-ing for, I can maybe narrow it down. You have to remember I see y'all day in and day out, so I more or less know a lot of people's schedules."

Leaning back and scratching his chin he thought for a second. "What about Miss Alexandria?"

One of Jeff's eyebrows raised. "The smoke show? Sure, she usually comes in at around eight or so."

"Why did you say 'usually?'"

"Because I was working yesterday morning and specifically remember her coming in early. If we pull up the tape here," he said, minimizing the current file and pulling up an earlier one. "Give me a second here to rewind. It would be at the very end of the video because she was the last car to come in for at least fifteen minutes or so until Janet drove up."

Moving the mouse back to when Jeff and Alexandria had their ten second conversation, he paused the video.

"Tell me exactly what you said and exactly what she said." Jack leaned back, staring into Jeff's soul, hoping to get some sort of clue to help him in this investigation.

"I said, 'isn't it a little bit early for you to be in right now,' she said, 'yeah, well if you want to get work done around here you have to beat everyone to it' or something like that."

Looking back at the screen, Jack said, "Okay, now can you track her through all of the footage for the next thirty minutes or so?"

"Why don't you give me something harder to do?" Jeff said. After pressing some buttons, he right-clicked on her car. Everywhere the car went, the video cameras would pull up automatically without needing Jeff to touch anything. The cameras continued to track her when she stepped out of the car and walked through the building to her office.

Looking at his watch, Jack's stomach growled. "Can we speed this up, bud, I haven't eaten since breakfast."

"Yeah, give me a sec," he said, moving the mouse and clicking a button labeled with the number one and an X next to it. Speeding up the video just a bit, both men watched her enter her own office, drop off her bags and throw away her drink before she exited her office.

"Okay, slow it down," Jack asked. Jeff complied. "Where are we going, Miss Alexandria," Jack said underneath his breath. Suddenly, the video screen went dark.

"What the hell just happened?"

"That, my friend, is a very good question." Restarting the video, and taking off the follow feature, Jeff pulled up the individual video files for each camera and both men watched as the exact same thing happened. As soon as she left her office, the video went black.

"Jeff, who else has access to these files?"

"All of the supervisor shift chiefs, so four in all. I will always have access, obviously, because I run everything down here, but only the chiefs of whatever watch they're assigned to have access to these tapes."

"Do you trust them all?"

"With my life," Jeff responded, who now had a sense of annoyance in his voice. "You'll have to excuse me if I sound upset, but I know it's not my guys who would erase any of these files."

"So, you're thinking it's foul play on my end somewhere?" Jack asked.

"Either that or someone from the outside managed to hack into our system, which wouldn't make any sense because if they could get through the impenetrable firewalls, etc., then why just stop at erasing that video file? Why not go after personal information and other stuff?" Jeff asked, his brain working in overdrive trying to figure out how someone hacked into the files without his knowledge.

"Dammit."

"What?"

"There's a lot of hackers out there, but only a handful of people who I know that are capable of hacking into databases like ours without a trace, and one of them doesn't live too far away."

CHAPTER 31

It was a quarter past their meet time and Preston Anderson was running late. Alexandria hated it when people arrived late. Growing up in a household with strict parents who had a military background, she quickly learned that on time meant you're late and arriving early meant you're on time. She had arranged the money transfer at the local bar, The Mountain Top, named because the owner climbed Mount Everest.

Happy hour began thirty minutes prior, and she was on her second Mojito when she saw an overweight man with a pimple-ridden face stumble through the door. Wearing a Call of Duty short-sleeved shirt and jeans smeared with pizza all over them, he made his way over to her. Lowering her baseball cap over her face, trying to hide that she was remotely associated with this man, she looked down into her drink. Luckily, she snagged the last high top in the back of the semi-crowded bar so less people would see them together—or so she thought.

As Preston sat down across from her, giving her a gentle shit-eating grin, she slid the thin happy hour menu over toward him with the money in a small envelope underneath. "I heard the Moscow Mule is really good," she said.

Grabbing the menu from the bottom and quickly shoving the envelope in his pocket, he replied, "Yeah, I do like a good Moscow Mule from time to time."

The waitress walked over to take Preston's order and walked back to the bar. "You look nice," he said, noticing her stunning figure in yoga pants and a tank top.

"Save it," she said. "I'm literally here for as long as I finish this Mojito, and then I'm leaving. You know the drill," she said as she put the tall glass to her lips and taking two big gulps. The waitress walked back over, dropping Preston's drink off with a polite smile.

"You know, you might do better with attracting women if you dressed, you know, like a normal person," Alexandria said in a condescending tone.

Preston responded, "Careful now, you can't talk like that when you go to prison."

"You idiot, if I go, you go, that's how this works. And that's what I'm paying you for, to make certain things disappear so that *we* don't have to go to prison," she said, pointing to the both of them.

"Ohh, that's a very good drink," said Preston, ignoring her. "You know, I've been in this business a very long time, a lot longer than you have. I have watched people go to prison for the work that I have done for them and yet here I still stand."

"You know, if you're so good at IT work, why don't you get a legitimate job somewhere and make an honest living?" she asked, taking another long gulp of her drink.

"Because I like doing what I do and I hate working for people. It doesn't get simpler than that. As far as your video file, that was an easy fix. I just had to—"

"Listen, I don't want to know how you did it and quite frankly I don't care, just as long as you are one-hundred-percent certain that it's done," interrupted Alexandria, disgusted more and more the longer she sat. The occasional feeling of a million beady eyes behind her, and her taking small shots to check, confirmed her earlier suspicious of people staring at the two of them. God forbid they thought they were a couple.

"It is. Trust me."

"How can I trust you when you just told me you watched people go to prison for what you do on the reg?" She sat back in her
chair watching his long dark hair fall over his eyes.

"Not *everybody* has been to jail, it's just the ones that don't *listen*. What you asked me to do is very easy and I can do that in my
sleep, no problem. Even some of the things that you have asked
me to do in the past like erase emails from people, hack into bank
accounts, etc.—however, that's just the tip of the iceberg. You forget that we're in D.C. This is a political town and it pays to know
the right people when you have to run for office." He finished his
sentence with a big smile exposing his yellowish teeth.

She winced at the sight of his teeth. Looking at her glass
one more time and downing the rest of the alcoholic drink, she
slammed it down on the wooden table. "It appears that our time is
up." She slid her barstool back and grabbed her purse.

"That's fine," he responded. "I'm meeting some friends here
anyway."

"You have friends?" She said, raising her eyebrow and slinging
her purse over her shoulder.

Chuckling softly, he said, "Yes, even though I am an evil person who does jobs for people that are completely illegal, I do have
friends."

Shaking her head in disgust, she gave her hacker acquaintance
one last pity smile and made her way to the front door. If she were
more aware of her surroundings, she might have noticed a familiar
figure sitting just to the right of the door on one of the barstools
that looked out onto the street.

CHAPTER 32

Making sure he heard the door close and adding a good five minutes in case she forgot something and came rushing back, he neatly folded up his newspaper and stuffed it underneath his arm. Grabbing his Irish coffee and offering up his seat to the couple that just entered the bar, he made his way back to where Alexandria was just sitting.

"Preston Anderson," Jack said, setting the paper down first and then his drink before grabbing his seat. Jack smiled after seeing Preston's 'oh-shit' look creep across the young hacker's face. "Oh, this seat is still warm. Why do you think that is, Preston?"

"I don't know, Jack," he said, his voice shaking a little.

"Are you in a rush? It's been a while since we've seen each other, hasn't it?"

"Yep, and I'm meeting some friends here in a little bit, so whatever it is that you want to talk about, can you speed it along please?" he asked.

A feeling of euphoria grew over Jack in knowing he had this man flustered by his presence alone. Toying with people of his nature was one of his favorite pastimes. He and Preston went back a couple of years to when Jack was tasked with following a mole who David believed was somehow taking funds from the agency's financial stream. The trail led him to Preston. Confronting the hacker, Jack realized that his abilities could be better suited if he needed a favor instead of twiddling his thumbs behind bars. Stipulations were implemented and Jack pulled a lot of strings to keep him out of jail.

"Don't worry, I won't keep you long, Preston. I just want to know why the seat is still warm, that would imply that someone was sitting here before me, correct?"

Giving him a straight face and showing no expression, Preston said, "You know exactly who was sitting there, and if you're over here talking to me, then obviously you found something on her."

"Not necessarily, but thank you for telling me that it was a woman. I don't think that you would last two seconds on the stand in court, do you?"

"You've made your point."

"What did she pay you for?"

Chuckling softly and feeling a bit bullied, Preston answered, "Who said I was paid for anything? I just happened to meet a friend. We chatted for a bit, and she left. And now, like I said, I am meeting old friends to discuss some video games."

"Cut the crap, Preston. Or do I need to contact the Federal Bureau and let them know I found the missing connection to the financial crisis case last year?" He watched Preston squirm, looking over both shoulders to make sure nobody was listening.

Leaning toward Jack, Preston's facial expressions turned serious. "Look, all she wanted me to do was delete some video surveillance files from your database, that's it. I swear."

Raising an eyebrow, he said, "And is that all?"

"Jack, I swear that's it," he replied, raising both hands in the air as if to offer a surrender.

"Preston, why don't you get a real job where they will pay you for your abilities?"

"Damn, that's the second time I've heard that today. I don't know," he said, now looking into his empty mug. "I guess I owe some people some money and I'm almost done paying them back."

Giving him a disappointing sigh—because Jack knew the agency would prosper greatly from his technology abilities—he said, "Hurry up and pay them back, because I would prefer you work with us, not against us."

"Really?" he asked, as Jack stood up and grabbed his newspaper. "What about my background?"

"What background? Maybe if you come on over to the good side we can make certain things disappear that happened in your past. Have a good evening, Preston. And next time you erase video footage from the agency, I'll put the cuffs on you myself." Jack made his way out of the bar and off to give Janet the information he just acquired.

CHAPTER 33

Max was fast asleep when he felt a tap on his shoulder. As his eyes struggled to adjust to the black figure in tactical gear and baklava staring back at him, he looked at his watch. "What is it? It's three in the morning, Antonio."

"Amigo, I need your help," he responded, not bothering to whisper and waking up the rest of the team. "We have a situation. Some of my men are down with food poisoning, so I need to borrow you guys to take their spot."

"What kind of situation?" Max asked, sitting up. Moving his neck in small circles, he tried to loosen up the stiff muscles all over his body.

"One of our informants on the street said that Alejandro is sending one of his subs into the river today from the middle of the rainforest. If he makes it into the river, the chances of us finding it shrink drastically. If it makes it to the ocean, then we'll never see it again."

Narco-trafficking around the world was a gigantic issue. It brought billions of dollars to cartels especially since there was no area where they were not willing to extend their reach. For decades South American countries, who didn't have corrupt political parties, worked with the United States trying to stop speed boats, fishing boats, airplanes, cars and any other conveyance. The hardest to stop, or find for that matter, was a fully submersible submarine floating around in the middle of the ocean. It was a needle in a haystack.

"How many openings are there into the ocean from the river they're using?" Alex asked, sitting up in his cot and joining Max in the conversation.

"There's only one, *amigo*," replied Antonio, looking at his watch.

"When do we need to launch?" Alex asked.

"Fifteen minutes."

"Perfect," Max responded.

"I take it we don't have an option of sleep, do we?" Kyle asked. Even though he couldn't see her because the lights were still off, he felt Courtney's beady eyes piercing his soul.

"Stop being a lazy ass," she said. "It's too early for your comments."

"Jeez, rough crowd," he said, throwing off his blanket and standing up to stretch.

"Well," Antonio said again. "I only need two to three of your guys."

"You already know I'm in," Max said, standing up and yawning as he followed Kyle in stretching to help increase the blood flow.

"I'm in, too," Alex said.

"Since Kyle needs his beauty sleep," Courtney said, "I'll go, I want to see this for myself. I've never seen one of the drug subs. I've only heard about them."

"Perfect," Antonio said. "Three's company, as you Americans say," he said, patting his friend on the shoulder and walking out of the room. Antonio turned around one last time and said, "Fifteen minutes, then meet by the elevator."

The team didn't have time to do anything but use the bathroom, throw their carriers on, and top off their weapons. Night raids was the realm in which Max lived. Seeing the element of surprise in the enemy's face was the best part, right before they caught his bullet between their eyes or a knife to the throat. Some might say he was kind of weird for thinking that way, but he didn't care, he was good at what he did and he knew it.

Walking to the elevator, Max noticed Antonio talking to one of his operators as he turned around to pat him on the shoulder again.

"Awake yet?" he asked.

"I know its dark outside, so just focus on not shooting me in the back please."

"Aha! Very funny my friend, just remember you need our helicopter to take you back here *pendejo*. It would be a shame to leave you behind, accidentally." Finishing his sentence in air quotations, Max was silent. Typical banter between operators, he loved it.

Antonio led the first group—which consisted of Max, Courtney, Alex and a few more of his men—to the roof. Exiting the elevator, Max winced at the noise emulating from the engines of the two Blackhawk helicopters as their blades picked up speed. Taking off his ballcap, Max stuffed it into his cargo pants pocket and followed Antonio and the rest of the team jogging over to the first Blackhawk.

Piling into the bird, Max was the last man to pick up the headset and plug in the cord connected to the communication system. He pulled the door shut, but Antonio signaled for him to open it back up, as one of his men shifted the mounted M240 machine gun from inside the cabin to being exposed outside.

There were only two cords, not including the gunner's, allowing the passengers in the cabin to talk to each other and communicate to the pilots. Max and Antonio were using them both. Everyone else would just have to make facial gestures, hand signals, or borrow the cord from whomever was using it if they wanted to say something.

Max took a gander at the M240 machine gun and its operator sitting to his right. Typically, Antonio had the guns and running on both sides, but one of the guns went down in each helicopter so making do with the cards dealt was a regular occurrence. Max realized he had never been in a situation where he had to engage threats from the sky but was overwhelmed with a sense of security. "I take it you've had to use those big boys on more than one occasion?" he asked Antonio.

"Yes," responded Antonio.

"Damn," Max said. The level of confidence he picked up from his response secured his faith in the operation. He was so used to being in control of where his weapon was pointed, when he would pull the trigger, and who was watching his back. In the sky, flying around at a couple thousand feet, he was at the mercy of literally everything else. It had been a while since he had flown in a helicopter. Most of his missions involved him jumping out of planes at an extreme altitude or taking some form of undercover vehicle to the destination.

Seven people occupied the cabins per helicopter not including the gunners. Two benches occupied the cabin on both sides, as Courtney and Alex sat to his left, while Antonio and his men were directly across from them. Exposed wires dangled all around them in unison with the oil dripping sporadically above. Max was all too familiar with the classic saying, "if the oil stops dripping, then there's something wrong."

The gunner checked his loadout one last time before giving the all-clear to the pilots. Adjusting his eyes to the darkness beyond the rooftop, Max felt a feeling of nervousness mixed with euphoria creeping across his body as the helicopter gently rose into the early morning sky. As they hovered while the pilots checked the parameters of their craft, Max gripped the handlebar attached to the door frame above him. Even though all the passengers wore a five-point harness, the shock of falling out always overcame whatever emotions were swimming around in Max's brain.

The warm air breeze flowing through both open doors of the cabin comforted Max, but only a little. The ride to the location would take approximately thirty minutes, and the hike to the location was another thirty or so, which wasn't terrible. Not a bad way at all to start the morning Max thought, even though the raid to save Ben would happen that night.

The helicopters gained altitude in unison, cutting their way through the sky. The higher they climbed, the colder it got. Goosebumps engulfed Max's exposed arms, causing him to shiver the second they reached their cruising altitude. He wished he had thrown on the long-sleeved shirt he packed.

The next half hour, he hugged himself, trying to keep warm, and thought of sitting back on the beach in Miami, drinking a cocktail and hitting on women. But even he knew that life would only keep him happy for so long.

Approaching the landing zone at five minutes out, Antonio spoke. "Okay, so me and my men will go down the rope first, secure the area. You guys follow. The second bird will give us cover and when we hit the deck, this one will break off and repeat the process."

"Roger that," Max responded, lowering his BNVD PVS-15 night-vision goggles and clicking the side button, illuminating the dark sky into white phosphor. Adding to the easiness of night shooting, their rifles were equipped with Infrared strobes, making the laser visible to the goggles when the IR button was engaged. It was typically described as playing a first-person shooter.

Lowering its altitude, the Blackhawk reached a steady one hundred feet as the second helicopter went into a holding pattern. Max watched Antonio attach the rope to the arm that extended out of the helicopter, ensure his gloves were on tight, grip the rope, and slide out of view.

One by one Antonio's men disappeared and before he knew it, Alex and Courtney had slid out of view also. Max unplugged from the helicopter and slid over to the rope. Gripping it and wrapping his legs so the rope sat on top of the bottom boot and underneath the top, he flew down the rope.

His training instantly kicked into gear and all he could remember was the general misconception that everything came from upper arm strength. It was in fact the legs that controlled the descent, the arms just keeping you attached. Before he knew it, his feet tapped on solid ground. Quickly jumping out of the way, he took up a defensive posture next to Antonio, kneeling approximately five yards in front of him. Max heard the rope detach and hit the ground behind him as the second helicopter flew in to deliver its payload.

Max's legs and arms screamed in agony, and he could sense a massive headache growing as well. The sleep helped a little, but he would have to ask Antonio for some painkillers after another hot shower if they were going to hit Alejandro's mansion later. Pushing future mission planning thoughts from his head, he focused back to the current task at hand.

"Last man,"

"Roger that," Antonio said. "Let's keep comms quiet, we don't need to let mother nature know we're here. There's scarier things in the Amazon than people carrying rifles."

Lowering his rifle, reaching into his pocket, and putting on his hat, Max responded. "We just flew two Blackhawks over her canopy, I'm sure she knows we're here already."

"Smart-ass," Antonio responded, "you know what I mean."

"Okay then, after you," Max said.

CHAPTER 34

Max was happy to be following the lead of Antonio, he needed a break from being the point man. He loved being in charge and calling the shots, but this mission was starting to take a toll on him and if he had to hear one more comment out of Kyle's mouth, he was sure he would kill him on the spot. And he knew Jack would help him cover it up.

Trekking at a slow yet consistent pace, they hadn't made it ten minutes before Antonio paused, raising up his arm.

"Tango," he whispered, "one o'clock, fifteen yards." Instantly the entire group lowered to their knee as two of Antonio's men took aim on the target. It took a second for Max to spot the target, but once he did, he trained his rifle on him as well.

All fourteen operators had spread out behind Antonio creating a small half-circle extending fifteen yards. The target appeared to be squatting in front of a bush with his back to the group.

"Standby," Antonio said again. "I want this one." Both of his men lowered their silenced rifles as Antonio crept to the target, watching his step over loose branches and crisp leaves with the possibility of giving away their position.

Max watched his beloved friend move his rifle behind him, reach for his blade, and pull it from the sheath strapped across his chest. Antonio, now less than ten yards away, adjusted the grip so the blade was facing upwards toward the sky. Thirty seconds seemed like an eternity from Max's viewpoint. Pausing right behind the bush, Antonio sprung like a king cobra raising its upper body and lashing downward to immobilize its prey. Antonio's left hand grabbed the man's mouth as his right simultaneously thrust the knife into the man's throat. He was dead in an instant.

Noise ceased to exist as one of Antonio's men quickly pushed forward, stepped around the bush, and grabbed the lifeless body, placing it on the dirt.

Walking up to him, Max smelled it before he even said anything. "Damn, bro, you killed him when he was taking a shit? At least let the poor man finish first."

Smiling, he replied, "Bro, he was in the middle of pushing one out, too."

"You're something else, man. A normal person doesn't get off on that kind of crap," Max said, watching Antonio wink and blow him a kiss, then signal for them to engage their walk again.

"If he walked this far out here to take a dump that means we're getting pretty close," Antonio mentioned to the rest of the group. "Keep a sharp eye out for any stragglers."

For the next twenty minutes the operators moved forward at a snail's pace to cover the remaining ground. Luckily, moving upwards in elevation with their target at the bottom of the ridge meant they could see the entire campsite and figure out the best plan of attack. Max's nerves were on high alert, his senses moving at full throttle. Not seeing any more random tangos in the area sent a wave of chills through his body, prepping himself mentally for what was waiting for them on the bottom of the ridge.

As the tree line subsided and nothing more was in front of them anymore except the edge of the ridge, Antonio knelt and whispered for everyone to do the same. "Okay, Courtney you're up," he said.

Without hesitation she grabbed the drone out of her backpack and set it up once more to do a fly by. The entirety of the group stayed in the tree line except for Max, Antonio, and Jose, the sniper. They all lay sprawled out on their stomachs at the edge of the ridge.

"You see anything good?" Max asked, who held out his hand taking the binoculars away from Antonio.

"There's that fence that wraps around the entire property, although it doesn't look like any barbed wire is on top of it so that's good. Worse comes to worst, we can scale it, although that's last resort. You see how they don't have any watchtowers, only four big tents?"

"Yeah, it's amazing how they assemble all this stuff in the middle of the rainforest," Max commented.

"Shoot, they could probably run their own car facility out here if they really wanted to," replied his friend.

"You're not wrong. I see the four tents and a hangar over the water, which is where I imagine the submarine is."

"Yeah, we hope it's in there," Antonio said, now sounding a little worried at that they couldn't physically see what was inside the hangar.

"Do you not trust your source?"

"I do," Antonio said, "but they've been wrong before. They could have reported it at the time and the cartel could have changed their location by the time we arrived on scene."

Giving the binoculars back to his friend, Max put some chewing gum into his mouth and offered Antonio a piece, which he obliged. "Don't worry, Courtney will find it if it's in there. That drone has a thermal mode on it that can pick up anything, even if it's under thin enough material. And I promise you, that material isn't thick enough to prevent a heat signature."

"I hope you're right, my friend," Antonio said letting out small sigh. "Max, I'm going to be completely honest right now, I'm getting tired of doing this out here. I feel like all of our efforts are in vain and sometimes they're not appreciated."

"Didn't you just tell me yesterday that because of your operations, the cartel has backed off?"

"Yes, but it's the same thing day in and day out. We bust some cartel members and they go to jail, but for every one or two we bust, more pop up. We can't win this battle, and I'm just tired of doing this monotonous thing repeatedly."

"What are you saying?" Max asked, who turned his attention to his friend, who seemed to be venting to him. He could hear it in his voice. But for being someone in their early forties, he was in better shape than people half his age. Max thought he knew what was coming next and he knew the physical ability was there. He just had to get to him mentally.

"I'm saying I am going to put in my letter of resignation when after we take down Alejandro," Antonio said, letting out a second sigh, staring at the faint lights at the campsite below.

Max could see how doing this job could be frustrating and just like that, an idea surfaced in his head. "What if I put in a word for you and you come join the Bering Group?"

"You're serious?" he asked.

"As a heart attack. I initially took this on as a favor to Jack. I've been working alone for the longest time, but I think I'm starting to come around."

"I'd have to think about it. This lifestyle is all I know, and I've been doing this since I was eighteen. I'll have a decent pension to retire somewhere down here, away from Cartagena. I've never lived anywhere else and done any other type of work other than this counter-narcotics stuff."

"Please," Max said, "why are you acting like you're gonna to pass this up?"

He laughed and then asked, "What else does this Bering Group do?"

Turning to look back down at the camp below, Max responded, "Shoot and kill people," he said, "you know, the usual. Just let me know what you think before I leave," he said.

"I can do that." Antonio smiled.

"Okay," Courtney said, "the drone is back."

"You ready to do this?" Max held out a fist. Antonio hit his fist against his.

"Brother, I was born ready."

CHAPTER 35

After the group finished going over all considered plan of attacks, they split up into their respective groups. Max, Courtney and Alex descended down the right side of the cliff. It wasn't steep enough to use rock climbing gear but being careful to not cause unnecessary rocks that fell below was difficult, especially at night.

Antonio took the rest of his men and descended the left side while Jose and another operator stayed above to overlook the campsite from the top. With every step, Max knew that would be the one to cause the rocks to slide, but it never happened.

Once they reached the bottom of the cliff, the three operators knelt next to one another and waited until Antonio radioed in to tell them they made it down safely. As much as Max wanted to take off his NVG's and look up at the night sky just to admire the view, he knew he couldn't. It wasn't very often he was able to see so many stars at night without the ambient lights of a big city nearby. It was the small things on missions like this that he cherished.

Shifting his field of view from the stars to the objective at hand, he glanced over at his two counterparts who were scanning for threats beside him. He hoped to God this would go off without a hitch.

"Okay, Max," Antonio said, "we're ready when you are."

"No, my friend, this is your op," Max replied, "we're ready when *you* are."

"Just like old times, *amigo. Execute!*" Antonio whispered.

The primary objective was taking out the tents which Max was certain housed people. The subsonic rounds they carried were not like the movies; noise still escaped the barrel of the suppressed weapon, but it sounded more like a subtle handclap than anything else.

Allowing Courtney to take lead, Max and Alex followed. The team was stacked to the right side of the first tent, anxiously waiting to make entry. The tents were massive, about fifteen to twenty yards across and ten yards deep. They reminded Max of the prison camps in Syria. Pushing the horrendous memories of torturing his victims out of his head, he pushed forward. He wasn't trying to re-live those thoughts in the Amazon jungle—or ever again.

Courtney crept up to the entrance and scanned for threats. "Ready," she said, as Alex squeezed her tricep. Alex and Max flowed behind her into the tent. Courtney dug the left corner, Max flowed right, while Alex stayed in the middle, all pointing their rifles at the threats in front of them playing dominoes. Shocked, all three individuals made a grab for their respective weapons lying next to them but the infrared lasers with the NVG's made shooting all too easy.

In a matter of seconds, the muffled noises barking from their rifles spat 5.56 rounds at all three Hispanic men now lying on the ground or slumped over on the table. As they continued to push through the tent, there were nothing but beds lined up against either wall. Making it to the other side and checking underneath all of the beds, Max called it clear as they stacked back up on the entrance to push to the next tent.

"Remember, we can't afford rounds to be flying into other tents and possibly hitting our guys. So, make sure you don't miss," Max said.

Both teammates replied as they continued to flow left into the other tent. It was here they didn't encounter any enemies, just a mountain of cocaine packaged and ready to go. Max estimated at least twenty thousand kilograms, possibly more all in one location. "This makes it easy when they want to transport it, I guess," he said.

"Yeah, no shit," Alex said, picking up the small package to feel its weight. Weighing in at just over two pounds, he tossed one to Courtney who let it fall to her feet.

"What's the matter, you've never played hot potato before?" Asked Alex.

"Are you done playing games?" she asked, picking it up and tossing it back into the pile with the rest of them.

"I thought you said you had never seen a narco-sub before?" Alex asked.

"Yeah, idiot, a submarine, not a mountain of cocaine," she responded. Alex walked over to her, picked up the key and tossed it back into the pile.

"Okay, let's hold here," Max said. "You two, check the rest of the tent." Walking toward the entrance, he said, "Antonio, how's your end?"

"We're done with our second tent, what do you guys have?" Antonio responded.

"Just a couple of tangos in the first one but we hit the mother-lode over here with drugs, how about you?"

"We had about five tangos in the other tent and the same with drugs on our end. They're getting ready to ship out, I think. There are too many drugs in this location to just be sitting here. I wish I could be there when Alejandro gets notified that another one of his shipments was stopped." Antonio laughed.

"Same," Max replied. "You guys ready to push on the final target?" He was getting anxious. The faster that this mission was over, the faster he could go back and the team could plan some more and possibly get some more rest for later.

"I radioed the helicopters right just before you keyed me; they're on their way back. About ten minutes out, so we need to move," Antonio said. Max signaled for his team to stack up. Flowing out of the tent and moving left, intertwining with Antonio and his men to the dock, they all regrouped. That's when Max thought he heard something whiz behind him.

"Shit, Antonio," he said. Freezing the train, everyone knelt and once again took up defensive postures, scanning for threats.

"What is it Max? We're sitting ducks out here," Antonio said anxiously.

"Check on your boys on top of the hill," he said. Looking around through his goggles, he couldn't see any heat signatures or movement that would cause suspicion, but he knew a sniper round when he heard it. As if on cue, rounds exploded all around them.

CHAPTER 36

"Returning fire!" Max screamed as the team ran as fast as they could down the dock and into the opening that led inside the submarine hangar. Walking backward and shooting wasn't Max's strong suit, but desperate times called for desperate measures as he and Antonio tried their best to give covering fire to everyone sprinting into the hangar. Bright lights were everywhere in his goggles, quickly realizing that covering fire was useless as he turned, tapped Antonio and the pair ran with the rest of the team into the hangar.

Half expecting to walk into a gunfight inside, Max breathed a sigh of relief seeing four men dead, floating in the water next to their massive semi-submersible submarine. It had to be at least sixty feet long, but only half of it exposed, with the hatch on top wide open. They were getting ready to load this bad boy up and ship it off, Max thought.

Quickly realizing the hangar was literally just covering a U-shaped pier, he made very careful footwork, not wanting to fall in the water. The team spread out as Max pushed past everyone who were now scattered all over the dock. There was no cover at all and the only way in or out was the opening where the submarine was pointed or the entrance they just came through. The rounds constantly pinging off the hangar were extremely loud and obnoxious. Noise echoed everywhere.

"Anything from your boys on the ridge?" Max screamed, joining Antonio in lying on the pier and trying to not catch a round to the dome.

"Yeah, I can barely make them out, but they said they counted at least ten guys all around them, but they haven't been seen so they are stuck for the time being." Antonio responded, who had now pushed his NVG's up.

"This is bad," Max said, "how much longer before the birds get here?"

Looking at his watch, Antonio said, "Five minutes, and I told them to step on it."

"They need to do more than that," Max responded, pushing his goggles up as well. "We're not going to have three minutes before they start shooting other things that do more than just ping off the sides of the metal."

"What do you suggest we do?" Antonio asked, looking at the operators lying down all around the pier. It was nothing short of a miracle how none of them had been shot or killed.

Doing his own quick scan, Max came up with an idea. "What we need is a distraction," he told Antonio, yelling over the ridiculous noise. "Grab the C4."

Max watched Antonio call his guy over with the explosives backpack and hand him two long skinny items wrapped in an olive-green package.

Waving for Antonio to follow him, he slung his rifle across his back and quickly climbed onto the submarine and down the hatch. Without time to conduct a proper scan, he hoped that no last-minute human beings were sitting inside. He did a quick survey of what he had to work with, which was nothing but three compartments: one for what looked like sleeping quarters in the front, a massive common space with nothing where they were standing, and the engines in the back.

Walking to the back of the submarine, Max had somewhat of an idea what he was looking at, but he didn't necessarily know how to start the engines.

He heard a clank behind him as Antonio's boots hit the deck. "Can you start this thing?"

"Does a bear shit in the woods? Move over, *pendejo*," Antonio said, handing him the backpack at the same time.

"What am I supposed to do with this?" Max asked.

Giving his friend a raised eyebrow in confusion, he asked, "You mean to tell me all the crap you and Jack have done in the past and you've never handled C4?"

"I decided pretty much at birth that I wanted to keep all of my limbs and body parts."

"Well," Antonio started, turning back around to mess with the levers and buttons in front of him. "You're about to learn today. Open the backpack and grab the sticks."

"Great," Max said, kneeling down and pulling out the serrated pocketknife. He was all for jumping out of planes, chasing drug runners in the Amazon, getting into fist fights and shootouts with the world's worst terrorists, but he vowed to never handle explosives. That was his line, and he drew it deep in the sand.

He had never officially done it himself, but seeing Jack do it enough in the field, he got the gist. Gently pressing the blade against the plastic package surrounding the explosives, he sliced a thin line down the length, exposing the white putty-like substance underneath. Removing the rest of the plastic and doing the same to its partner, he wiped the knife off and re-holstered it.

"Now what?"

"Grab the blasting caps out of the bag," Antonio said as the engine roared to life. Max grabbed the skinny silver-like tubes from the front pocket of the bag just as Antonio knelt and snatched them from his hands. "If you want stuff done right, you have to do it yourself. I got this. Get out and when I say so, untie the submarine from the pier."

"Roger," Max said, hustling back to the small ladder and hurrying out of the submarine. The rounds bouncing off the sides of the hangar re-engaged his mind the second his boots hit the pier.

"Okay, now!" he heard Antonio shout from inside the submarine.

Quickly running to the front and aft ropes keeping the sub attached to the pier, he removed them and by the time he was done with the aft, he witnessed Antonio climbing out.

The sub started moving forward as Antonio grabbed Max and pulled him as far back away from the submarine as possible.

"I think we have about a minute," he said. Just then the noise around them ceased.

"What?" Antonio screamed into his earpiece. "You're breaking up."

"They're moving down the hill." Max shared the same look of panic.

"Give me people covering that entrance," Antonio screamed to his men as they scrambled to get up and get in a good position to destroy anything that entered. The rest of the men, including Courtney and Alex, stayed prone on their stomachs, covering the shore to the left of what they could see outside. As the submarine was now halfway sticking outside of the hangar, Max was right on all accounts as rounds pinged off the top of the grayish hull.

The shooters were close, because Max could now hear screaming from someone outside, probably from the person in charge. He couldn't make out what they were saying but the shooting stopped, so whoever was doing the screaming obviously didn't want to destroy their boss's property.

"Standby!" Shouted Antonio. In the next couple of seconds the submarine erupted in an enormous fireball, simultaneously blowing a hole in the top of the hanger.

"It doesn't seem like any more tangos around us," overwatch stated. "We count twenty or so total."

"About damn time, where have y'all been!" Antonio screaming into the headset.

"They were all around us *jefe*, standby."

Just then the distant unmistakable thumping of two Blackhawks could be heard overhead as the cycle of mounted automatic weapons were fired. Although they couldn't see anything from their positioning inside the hangar, Max knew all too well what the carnage would look like on the other end of the guns pouring out lead into whoever was unlucky enough to be on the receiving end of them.

Listening to the spent casings now clanking off the roof of their building, Antonio's men stood up and cheered. In a matter of seconds, the all-clear came across the headsets from overwatch.

CHAPTER 37

Ben was in a bit of a conundrum. On the one hand he was now officially a bodyguard to one of the most well-known drug lords in the world. If Alejandro Alvarez died, so did his immediate family. On the other, if Ben tried to run, then his family died. There was no way out. Not if, but when Jack sent the team, he would have to defend Alejandro. It was the only way, for now.

The good news was, Alejandro gave him free reign to walk around his massive mansion because he thought he had him wrapped around his finger. Somehow, he would have to play that card to his advantage when the proper time arose.

Now that he was an active bodyguard, he was given the same privileges as the other guards, in addition to new clothes to wear. Ben was no longer locked away in his room, although his barren dungeon of a room was still where he was required to stay. He couldn't give up even though he was one of the washouts—Jack saw something in him that he wanted and believed in, so now it was up to him to dig deep and pull whatever he saw in him out of his ass and go to work, somehow.

Throwing on his new black slacks and polo, one size too big, he walked downstairs into the kitchen and saw Alejandro on the phone. Judging by his stern voice, he was not happy. Alejandro gave him a look of death and pointed to the veranda. Ben quickly found out: as long as it was a sunny day, they would be eating all of their meals there. Saint Bertrand wasn't just the name of the cartel, he was the saint the entire cartel believed in, the saint they put their trust in, and the saint they confided in when times got rough.

It was by his name the cartel had survived and had accumulated so much wealth over time—or so that's what Alejandro wanted to believe and credit all his success to.

Sitting down at the table where a man was murdered just days ago, Ben remembered the blood splattering against the tile. Pushing the horrible memory out, he grabbed a seat and waited for his new boss to walk outside. In the background, Ben could hear yelling and something shattering on the ground. Great, he thought. Thirty seconds later Alejandro joined him, pulling up and sitting next to him. Both men sat in silence as the butler brought out some coffee and water for them. Ben could feel his heart jerk once more, because he saw firsthand how dangerous this man was. The last thing he wanted to do was get on his bad side. After taking a sip of his coffee and crossing one leg over the other, Alejandro initiated the conversation.

"It appears that a team has blown up one of my facilities in the jungle."

Thinking of the right words to say, even though he was ecstatic on the inside, he said, "I'm sorry to hear that."

Shooting Ben a blank stare and shaking his head, he responded, "No, no, you're not. You would love nothing more than for all of this to be taken from me and for you to be whisked away back to where you came from."

Taking a large gulp of coffee before he responded, he said, "Yeah, I'm not going to lie."

Setting his coffee glass back on the table and looking down over the valley, Alejandro said, "Of course. However, I have many more facilities, but this load was supposed to go to a major supplier and now I have to make some phone calls and fix it."

Looking behind him to his right, he waved Pablo over and whispered what he wanted done. Pablo briskly walked back into the house to finish whatever task was given to him.

"Do you know who it was?" Ben asked. He knew all too well what went into blowing up a cocaine facility in the middle of the jungle.

"I have an idea, however, if I was being honest about it, I don't know. But I did have reports of two black helicopters leaving the scene and some *wedo's* were with them. Just remember, Ben," Alejandro said, turning to him as a butler dropped off their meal for the morning.

"I get it, Alejandro," snapped Ben in response, watching the drug lord chuckle.

"Oh, but don't worry," he said, biting into his toast, "your dad will be made to watch as well."

CHAPTER 38

Jack told Janet he had some information on their lead, so she met him at the mansion, safe and clear from prying eyes and ears. She was only in the house for ten minutes before Jack was grilling steaks for them to eat while they figured out what to do about their problem. It was still technically a workday and although they were at a safe and secure within the confines of the mansion, miles from Langley, they both could be called back to the agency for any number of reasons, so water was the best choice as far as drinks went to accompany the T-bones that Jack brought back into the house.

As soon as the steaks entered through the sliding glass doors, the smell caused Janet to salivate. He set the steaks on top of the stove, stepped back outside to grab the asparagus, and closed the door behind him. Jack would have loved more than anything to eat outside and admire the weather and warm breeze, but a conversation like this one needed to be conducted inside. They couldn't risk the off chance someone was monitoring them.

"Your plate isn't going to fix itself," Jack said smugly. She finished texting on her Blackberry and noticed how serious he was. She stood up to grab her food. After grabbing some waters, the two sat down as Janet created conversation.

"Since you're out of the loop right now, I thought I'd let you know they're going to hit the compound sometime tonight."

Jack looked up from his steak. "About damn time."

"I want you to take the jet to Austin this afternoon so you can personally give Ben's parents the news when we get him."

"And on the off chance we don't?"

"Then you still deliver the news. Either way I'm sure you've done this before."

He didn't like the idea of delivering bad news, but somebody had to. "Fair enough, I'll leave when we're done."

"Now," she said in between bites, "what did you find?"

"It seems like your theory is correct," Jack said before biting into his medium rare cut.

Finishing a piece of asparagus and swallowing before she continued, she said, "What do you mean 'theory?'"

"It means that security has video evidence of her coming into work, walking to her office and the next thing they have is her returning to her office, nothing in-between."

Janet pointed her knife at Jack. "Bullshit, how do they not have footage of that? We're the most secure place in the country next to the White House and we can't even keep track of employees entering and leaving the building? That's some bullshit and you know it, Jack."

"Relax, Janet, I've known the guy who runs security longer than you have been employed here. He's a dear friend of mine and wouldn't do anything to jeopardize this agency. Trust me when I say they have no footage of her going into your office. All they have is what I just told you."

"Now what?" she said, putting another bite of steak into her mouth. The juices were dripping down the side of her mouth as she grabbed a napkin to wipe them away.

"Lucky for you, as I just alluded to, I have been in this business a very long time and have many connections around here."

She replied, "Yes, we all know you're the big man on campus. Spit it out Jack, what are you trying to tell me?"

"I found the man who was hired to erase the files."

"And how exactly did you do that?" she exclaimed while looking at her watch. "It hasn't even been twenty-four hours."

"Like I said, I have connections and like you just said, I'm the 'big man on campus,'" replying with air quotations. "Anyway, just know that I believe beyond a shadow of a doubt that it was her." He said between bites of asparagus.

"What do you propose we do?"

"Let's look at the bigger picture. We now have an agent who we think is leaking information—even though we don't know how much information—out to people who are not authorized to have it. If this gets out, the agency could be ruined, and the Bering Group will no longer exist because we're already on a tight leash as it is. We're supposed to be the wet work group that goes bump in the night and not only did we have an agent kidnapped, but now we have someone leaking files? Ms. Moore will have us shut down in a heartbeat to avoid the president finding out," Jack said.

"Between her and David, they can't make this magically go away?"

"There is no magically making this disappear. To cover all of our asses, Alexis would shut it down and David would re-rack all of us to different assignments. It would be the biggest bust of a CIA program in a very long time. He's the director and as much as we love each other, he absolutely cannot let this information get leaked to the press because you had better believe that this White House Administration does not play games like the last one. Plus President Howard isn't the biggest fan of David and the way he runs the agency. This may be the powder keg that causes all of us to lose our jobs."

They sat in silence and finished their meals while simultaneously thinking about how to resolve their issues. Janet was new to all of this and had never encountered anybody trying to steal information out of the agency, much less from her office. Jack, on the other hand, had been with the agency for just about two decades now and knew more than anything how stuff like this turned out.

There was more than one instance in the past where things like this had happened but more often than not, if it was kept in-house and not leaked to the press, then that was that. There was only one real way Jack knew more than anything to handle a situation like this, and as much as he wanted to just run with it, Janet was his boss now and he had to respect the chain of command. Since she came forward and wanted to sort of turn over a new leaf, he felt obligated only a little to have his idea approved and to bring her directly into his world of work.

"This has happened once or twice before. Not necessarily stealing information from an office, but agents in the field going rogue and having to be dealt with," Jack said, folding his arms across the table. "This doesn't end well, and quite frankly there is only one way out of this," he said, taking a sip of his water. "She has to disappear."

They continued to make small talk and finish their meals as Jack explained how the agency dealt with certain individuals in the past. To Jack's surprise, Janet's composure remained calm, cool, and collected as she finished her food and leaned back, letting out a long sigh. She looked around and admired the craftsmanship that went into building this mansion for their new group.

"You know, signing off on a project like this to build you guys your own fortress of solitude wasn't easy, but it would be a shame to see this go to waste. If the Bering Group gets dismantled over something like this, I will most definitely be out of a job. And finding one as good as this one, including the perks, is out of the question. I might as well be putting in my papers to work at a fast-food chain."

Scooting her chair back and grabbing her purse sitting next to her on the table, she turned to Jack. "I don't care what you have to do, but get it done." And with that, she left.

CHAPTER 39

After landing safely back at the police station, the team took the elevator back underground, taking showers then eating breakfast while filling in Kwame, Nate, and Kyle on what happened. When everyone was washed and fully satisfied with food, Max and Antonio gathered everybody who would be participating in the raid of Alejandro's compound later that evening in the conference room. As it turned out, Antonio had one more trick up his sleeve.

He had made a phone call while everyone was eating and taking showers, calling in a favor from one of his diplomatic friends who worked in directly for the Minister of Defense. Within two hours, twenty additional Special Forces personnel from the Colombia Army had joined them in the conference room.

Proper introductions came first, and the room was so crowded now that there was no room to even sit. The chairs had to be taken out to make way for everyone involved in the operation. Max and Antonio stood on either side of the big television screen at the end of the room which displayed a live satellite feed, courtesy of Janet, of Alejandro's mansion.

"Okay," Max said, raising his hand to quiet down the chatter of almost fifty people. Not only had Antonio made the call to the Special Forces, but every person who worked under Antonio was called in for this operation.

"As you can see," Max said, "on the screen is a massive complex. This is real time footage that is provided by a live drone circling the compound. To those of you who don't know, *we*," he said, pointing to the rest of the operators who came down with him, "are here specifically to get our buddy who was kidnapped by Alejandro and his organization." Clicking off of the video feed and clicking onto a picture of Ben, he said, "This is our friend Ben. We don't know exactly where he's being kept, so memorize this photo. Our primary goal on this mission is to extract him without incurring any more bumps or bruises along the way while helping you all with your cartel problem." Stepping aside, he let Antonio take over the presentation.

"Okay, raise your hand if you have not been to the compound," he said, clicking the button on the remote to re-engage the satellite imagery of the compound. Looking throughout the room, the only people who raised their hands were Max's team. Shaking his head at Max, who returned his look with a middle finger, Antonio continued. "We will have three teams. Arturo," he said pointing to one of the squad leaders of the Special Forces that walked into the room, "you will hit the compound by air at precisely 2300 hours tonight and land in the valley just below the compound." He pointed to the woods that surrounded the bottom portion of the screen that took up all of the space just below the empty soccer field surrounding the back of the mansion.

Nodding in response to his new tasking, Arturo gave a thumbs-up, as Antonio continued. "After we make entry, you guys will surround the property and will be responsible for three-sixty-degree security on the ground. Nothing leaves or enters without your permission."

"Nothing will come in or out of the compound while we are there," he said. Arturo looked like he would be the one scaring monsters in children's dreams. His tan and lean six-foot stature, his deep voice, and a scar reaching diagonally across his entire face was enough to cause people on the street to look the other direction. There wasn't a place on his arms that wasn't covered by tattoos. To any outsider not in the room, he looked the furthest from a federal officer.

Giving Arturo an approving nod, Antonio turned to his own men. "While Arturo and his men are jumping out of the plane at 2300 hours, the rest of us will be make our way up the dirt path to his compound at 2230. Once inside the compound, the rest of us will split up into two groups. The ones that went on the operation this morning will work with me and Max and help find Ben. When that task is complete, we will join Marco in the other group," he said, pointing to one of the lighter skinned operators in the room.

Max stepped in and said, "Nate, we could use you on that ridge overlooking his mansion."

"You got it," Nate said. "What do you guys use for sniper rifles down here? I didn't bring a long-range rifle with me, too much to carry for this mission."

"That's not a problem," Antonio said. "We have Barrett's."

"That's more than plenty," he spoke.

"You want some company?" Antonio asked.

"Sure, give me two shooters to watch my back and we'll call it even."

"Roger that."

A hand went up from one of Antonio's men. He pointed at him to allow him to speak, "Boss, what about his men? They'll have radios and when we start to drop these dudes, he's going to know something is wrong when they don't respond."

"Don't worry, we have that part taken care of," he answered, pointing to Max.

From here, Max took over the conversation. "We have a portable electromagnetic pulse emitter, courtesy of the United States government. The box knocks out any electronics, no matter what kind, within five hundred yards. We'll turn it on the second we suppress the first of the bodyguards at the bottom of the hill. If he has a generator to power up the house, it will have to be gas powered."

"You guys just carry that around with you when you go on missions? Won't that knock out our radios?" asked the same individual.

"Negative. We restocked on gear when we hit the safe house in Colombia, and as long as the radios are programmed to a certain frequency, we'll be fine. This is the newest in research and development," he said, seeing the same person about to ask a question again. "No, his men won't be running this frequency, trust me. We don't know what kind of state that Ben will be in. After we find him, we have to make sure he can get whatever medical attention that he needs ASAP. Me and my team will personally escort Ben to one of the helicopters outside, drop him off, then hightail it back to link up with the rest of you in the mansion. Any questions?"

Satisfied that no one said anything else, Antonio spoke up. "This will be a kill, not capture mission. He has escaped our grasp for the last thirty plus years, and now this is our chance to make a change for this country. When tonight is over, we will pick apart his organization piece by piece. He has infested the world with so much narcotics and developed an empire the likes of which no one has seen since the eighties and nineties. Tonight it ends, and there's no coming back."

CHAPTER 40

Jack hopped on the Gulfstream G550 with his bag packed and ready to go about an hour after Janet left after their lunch meeting. He was dead tired from the constant worrying about his team and finding out who snuck into Janet's office. Now he had to figure out a way to break the news to a family whose son was kidnapped and hopefully not killed. Well, he thought, his job would be so much easier if he managed to stay alive during all of this. Shaking his head, he closed his eyes and managed to take a couple of long breaths. He felt the jet engines screaming to life as they taxied out onto the runway.

Thinking about his late wife, Joanna, always brought him rest and relaxation. What would she be telling him right now? Why did he have to go deliver the news? Couldn't someone else go and take care of that simple task? He was far too old. Didn't he start this team with the ability to sit behind and watch from afar? He loved her and she was always supportive of him, but she didn't understand.

She was a yoga teacher when they first met and in the process of setting up her own studio. Neither of them wanted kids, and to be honest, it was for the best, especially with Jack's line of work. He loved his job and of course would have sacrificed everything for her if she truly wanted them, but she also grew up an only child and that's all she knew. Jack had brothers and sisters and kept in contact with them pretty frequently, but they all thought he was in the realm of finance. Jack saw day in and day out the labors and constant sacrifices his brothers and sisters had to make to get their children to soccer practice, school, dental appointments, etc., on time, and he wanted nothing to do with it.

As the jet climbed in altitude, he looked at his watch. He had a little while before he got there. Pushing away any bad thoughts creeping out of the dark crevices of his mind, he decided he would think about what to say in case the worst happened whenever the time came. But for right now, he would be no use to anyone if he didn't get some sleep.

Jack awoke as the jet touched down. The roar of the engines slowed as the aircraft approached the hangar. Giving a nice little stretch, he unbuckled his seat belt, and let his eyes adjust to his surroundings.

As the plane came to a full stop, he stood up and reached into the overhead compartment. He pulled out his bag, set it on the floor, and closed the compartment. Kneeling, he felt his knees give subtle pops. Stretching more often would be beneficial. He reached underneath his seat and felt for the black lever. He pulled forward on it, throwing the seat onto its back, exposing a hidden compartment. Underneath was an assortment of different weapons from short-barreled bull-pup shotguns, AR pistols, and regular pistols to a couple of stun-and-flash grenades. He grabbed a flash grenade to accompany his Springfield XD's and two extra magazines.

Adjusting the seat back to its original position, he noticed the pilot come out of the cockpit and give him a wave. "I see you guys still keep the liquor cabinet stocked?" he said, referring to the compartment he was just looking at.

"Of course, courtesy of Mr. David," said the pilot, who didn't look a day over forty. The pilot told Jack they had orders to wait in the hangar until he returned. Jack exited the plane via the drop-down stairs after the pilot pointed to his rental at the entrance to the hangar. Jack thanked them both for the smooth ride and walked over to the white, fully loaded Chevy Impala. Not bad, he said to himself. Opening the driver's side door, he tossed his day bag into the passenger seat, put his gun and other things he grabbed on the seat with it, and punched the hotel into the GPS.

CHAPTER 41

The convoy of four SUV's dropped Max and the rest of the operators off at the beginning of the dirt road leading to Alejandro's compound. The path was just barely big enough to fit a small SUV, and it was probably designed that way. Surrounding both sides were nothing but thick luscious trees that extended up the entire hillside as it curved all the way to the top. Using the video surveillance and information from Nate and his overwatch who were dropped off a couple of hours earlier and hidden on top of the ridge, they calculated the distance from the front of Alejandro's doorstep to the bottom of the ridge was approximately a half mile. Alejandro wanted to make sure he knew someone was on their way up his dirt road before they knocked on his front door.

"Heads up, there's a helo on top of the mansion. It definitely wasn't there in the video feed from earlier," Nate said.

As the group pushed into the trees, Max looked at his watch through his NVGs. 2230 hours. Knowing the second team would be lowering from the helicopter at this exact moment, he couldn't help but wish he was doing the same. He loved arial assaults because in his experience, it gave such a clearer glimpse of what the assault target looked like instead of some map or pictures presented most of the time.

The amount of personnel moving through the trees comforted Max. Everyone here was on board with taking down this horrible monster of a man. Dodging a low-hanging branch, he chanced a peek to his left and saw Kwame's gigantic figure doing his best to remain silent. Max couldn't help but laugh on the inside. At approximately one hundred yards, they encountered the first curve to the left, and just as predicted, three guards stood in the middle of the road with nothing but a couple of chairs to sit in. Max was just off to the left of Antonio as they both took point in this phase of the operation. Kneeling, they pointed their silenced rifles at their targets.

"Standby," Antonio whispered, "I'll take the one on the right."

"Roger," Max said, "I got the left then. Whose got the other one?" Max asked to anyone in general. With everyone assaulting the compound on the same frequency, things would get hectic soon as the mansion was breached, so teams coordinating with colors were created to help alleviate the issue. Max and Antonio made it absolutely imperative that communication was nonexistent unless absolutely necessary.

One of Antonio's men answered the call and when Max saw a third infrared beam on their last man, he waited until Antonio gave the count down. "Three, two, one." All three targets dropped simultaneously, as the team's rifles bucked and let their rounds do the talking.

"Targets down," Antonio whispered. Max and Antonio's group broke off and quickly secured the dropped targets, pulling their weapons off to the side of the road. Courtney reached into her backpack, pulling out the EMP device which was no bigger than a small external hard drive. It was the easiest thing in the world to operate as there were only two buttons, on and off. Clicking the 'on' switch and seeing a red blinking button showing it was working, she placed it back into her backpack. She brought her rifle back up to the ready position. Antonio grabbed one of the downed men's radios to listen to any communication going on within the mansion and moved to the opposite side of the dirt path.

A cool breeze caused Max to shiver just a little bit as he gripped his rifle a little tighter. It was a full moon, which wasn't the best for a surprise raid, but it was better than rain. Max's knees, quads, and calves were sore, as was his lower back. He was relieved they were finally walking up the trail to hit the mansion they flew all the way down here for. A massage was definitely in order when he arrived back at in Virginia.

As the team crested the hill, the full moon's extra light illuminated Alejandro's massive mansion. Just at the edge of the tree line, about fifty yards or so ahead, Max saw Marco and his group lying on their stomachs.

"Okay, standby," Antonio said, as the entire group knelt and used whatever brush or trees they had in their vicinity as cover.

"All good on my end," Max said to Antonio. "Just remember, when we get into the house, they have to watch their fire because there's no telling where Ben will be located."

Covering his mouthpiece, he said, "Don't worry, my old friend."

Whispering into his mic, he gave the clear for Marco's team to proceed as planned.

CHAPTER 42

The second the power shut down in the entire house, the backup gas generator kicked on, signaling to Alejandro that something was wrong. Pablo yanked Ben out of bed and told him this was where he earned his keep. Throwing on his quick uniform, Ben was ushered to meet Alejandro in the bedroom. It was here where Pablo left the two of them with two bodyguards outside of the room. Alejandro had added security measures to the mansion with raids from the police in mind, so he designed it knowing the only thing to knock out the power were extremely high winds and heavy rain.

Maintaining the deep, committed, and serious composure was all Alejandro had going for him right now. He knew his time was coming to an end. He had been raided before, but this time was different, and an uneasy feeling was developing inside the pit of his stomach.

The second he heard the submarine facility was up in flames that morning, in addition to gathering an abundance of extra men at his house, he made sure his personal helicopter was flown from his private airfield to his mansion. He wasn't about to go down without a fight.

"Should your buddies make it past all of my men, we're going to take this ladder and head to the roof. From there you and I are going on a trip to my private jet and heading to my other house in Spain."

"You have a house in Spain?" Ben asked.

"I'm not a billionaire because I make stupid decisions."

He listened in awe. This man literally had a plan for everything. Ben wasn't stupid, and although he didn't have the best covert and operating skills, he was smart enough to know what was going on, and knew someone was definitely coming. If not to save him, then to shut down Alejandro's entire operation.

Shutting the door behind them, Alejandro turned to Ben and gestured for him to take a seat. The room had a godawful maroon carpet with a small hatch in the corner of the room on the ceiling next to the ladder, and to its left were a couple of television monitors hanging from various points on the wall. At the bottom of the monitors were some controls with two chairs beside them. If an evil villain occupied a lair where he was going to monitor what went down on their island from a distance, this was it.

Grabbing one of the chairs, Ben plopped down and rubbed his eyes. He needed to wake up. If a time was going to present itself where he could try to escape, it was soon. The room was not that big, but then again, safe rooms weren't meant to be inhabited permanently.

The door opened back up with a couple of beeps and Pablo walked into the room with two assault rifles and some magazines. Handing one to Ben and one to Alejandro, he turned to Ben, giving him a death stare as if he were his son and royally pissing him off.

"*Maricon*, if anything happens to him," he said, pointing to his boss. Alejandro sho'ed him away, no longer needing to reinforce what he was sure Ben already knew. Ben knew exactly what torturous and heinous acts would be performed on him should Alejandro die.

The only thoughts racing through Ben's mind were how to escape with all of this chaos going on. Not wanting to upset Pablo further, who stood so closely he could smell the cigarettes on his breath, he gave him a quick nod, "Relax, I get it, dude," he said.

Pablo heard him, and left, shutting the door behind him. Glancing over at Alejandro sitting next to him, Ben saw the drug lord load his rifle and sit it on top of the control panel. Pulling out his cell phone, he dialed a number and placed it on speaker. The man whose voice picked up on the other end was familiar, and it only took a couple of seconds for it to register in Ben's head. In the blink of an eye a different facial expression overwhelmed Alejandro as he set the phone down right next to the rifle. It was the man watching over his mother.

CHAPTER 43

Jack was lucky the time zone in Texas was only an hour behind the East Coast. Looking at the clock in the car reading 8:00 pm, he was happy the operation down in Colombia was underway. The faster it began, the faster he could debrief Ben's parents hopefully with good news, and the faster he could get the hell back to Virginia. He was working off his second cup of coffee and managed to find a parking spot next to one of the houses that appeared to be having some sort of party—which meant that Jack's car would blend right in. As more cars arrived throughout the night, it only did more to help conceal Jack's cover of attending the party. Hearing faint music and smelling the familiar hotdog and hamburgers, brought him back to childhood memories. At least someone was having fun tonight.

Just as he was about to dive into his third podcast of the evening, he heard the slow rumbling of a white utility van driving past him, parking one house to the right from Ben's mothers. That's odd, he thought. The same pest control van was parked there when he first arrived. A coincidence, but Jack didn't survive this long in the business because of coincidences. When something registered as a red flag it usually meant something wasn't supposed to be there.

Gladly ending the history podcast on how Mussolini and Hitler treated their soldiers behind closed doors, he thought he would keep his attention focused on the van. At no point did he see anyone get out of it, but he did see a window roll down as a cigarette was being lit. The person inside tapped ashes onto the street. No,

Jack thought, this was someone who was clearly doing a stakeout on the house. Shooting a quick text to Janet he asked if she knew of any agency—maybe the local police department—watching over the house covertly making sure nothing happened. Replying in less than a minute, she said, "no."

Grabbing his one flashbang, his pistol and extra magazines, he threw on his hoodie and climbed over the passenger seat to exit on the sidewalk. Kneeling and pushing it softly closed, he wanted more than anything to see how many people were in the vehicle. It was hard to tell because the only windows that offered any sort of insight into the vehicle were on the driver and passenger sides of the car. Just as he thought about how he was going to approach the van, he heard the driver's side door open and watched as a Hispanic man with haggard jeans and a zip-up hoodie with the sleeves rolled up stepped outside and lean against the van.

"Dammit," he whispered. He thought he could make out tattoos all up and down the arms and face, but without any ambient light he couldn't be certain. The fact they were parked between the street-lights told him they at least knew somewhat of what they were doing.

Still kneeling behind the passenger side wheel well, he crept backward to the rear of the car and crab-walked back around to the beginning of the cul-de-sac where it met at an intersecting street. Making a right, he jogged lightly and tried his best not to attract any unwanted attention. As the street ended and poured onto one of the main roads behind the subdivision, he made another right, which brought him to a brick wall that ran the length behind the entire subdivision. Doing the math, he figured Ben's mom's house was only a little way down, and after judging which backyard he thought was the correct one, he took a couple steps back to make a running leap up the wall.

At age fifty-seven, he had to work out almost twice as hard to be able to keep up with the young bucks on his team, which was fine with him. They always gave him crap in the gym, but he would smoke most of them when they occasionally did their long distance running for fun. He loved his payback. The brick wall stood at seven to eight feet in height, and standing at only five foot seven, he would have to get a decent boost to grip the top of the wall.

Looking to his left and right and not seeing any cars, he rubbed his hands together as if doing so would create some sort of friction and went for it. His thin yet athletic frame allowed him to do things of this nature with ease, even at his age.

When he got enough momentum and his right leg was close enough to the wall, he used it to spring upward and made contact with the wall using his left leg. From there he very quickly brought his right leg upwards even higher than his left to help him climb the wall. As his right leg made contact with the wall, he pushed off, caught the top of the wall, and used whatever upward momentum he had left to help hoist himself quickly over it. Not knowing what was on the other side, he really had no choice but to take a leap of faith, literally, and hope for the best.

Jumping down to the other side, he stayed in a crouch position and ducked behind one of the bushes sitting in the corner. He was sure this was the right house. In the satellite imagery Janet gave him to look at while in his hotel room, he saw a pool and a small utility shed, which both were directly in front of him now. Looking around in case these people had floodlights that kicked on when motion was involved, he waited another minute before he shifting to the left. By his calculations, he needed to go two houses down to come up behind the van on the passenger side. Seeing a small wooden fence separating the yards, he rushed toward it, being as careful as possible to not make too much movement just in case someone randomly thought to look outside.

Scaling the last two fences that ran in a circular pattern to the left to match the cul-de-sac was easy enough. He made it to the last house and running the wall until he stopped at the left side of the house. A small wooden gate separated the front yard from the back, and he peered over it to look for the van. Just as he was about to open the gate, he heard a familiar noise behind him causing goosebumps to run the length of both arms.

CHAPTER 44

Nate, in conjunction with Marco's group laying in the trees, vectored each and every shot they took, wiping out the entire security section. When Nate and Marco saw no more men, Max motioned for everyone to crawl forward and merge with Marco's team lying at the tree line ahead of them. In a matter of two minutes, the both teams were sprawled across the tree line of the compound.

The driveway was massive, and sitting in the middle was a large stone fountain of a naked lady spewing water from her mouth back into the bottom of the fountain. Circling her was the driveway with a small assortment of beaten-up sedans and a couple of smaller motorcycles. The double doors stood directly in the center of the building right in front of the fountain, with a couple of stairs leading up to them. Massive pillars stood on either side of the double doors, extending up to the third and final floor of the mansion. To Max at a quick glance, it almost looked like some of the pillars in the Parthenon.

The gargantuan mansion stretched the entire length of the driveway and on either side of it was nothing but more trees. The hillside directly in front of the house on the other side of the driveway was so steep there was absolutely no way anyone was going to surprise this man. Except, of course, for Nate and his team already perched on top. Whoever came up with this design was very smart in the sense that the only logical way to reach Alejandro was straight up the skinny dirt path, and by the time they made it to the driveway, he would be ready.

"All good on my end. I mean, we all have to die at some point, my friend," Antonio said.

"I guess," Max replied. Crawling backward to Kwame, Kyle, and Courtney, he said, "Chances are Ben is upstairs in the master bedroom. Antonio told me earlier after the meeting that he has some sort of safe room located in the closet."

"Okay," Kwame whispered, scanning from left to right.

"Remember your training and y'all will be fine. You guys have never done anything of this caliber, have you?" Max asked, to which he got unanimous shaking of heads. "That's fine, stick to the plan and we'll all make it home. Watch each other's six in there, I can almost guarantee it's going to get hairy the second we make entry."

"Red team, check in," Arturo said over the earpiece.

"Roger, red team is good to go," Antonio answered.

"Roger, green team is in place, backyard secure. We had to deal with some wandering security but we're solid now. We have a nice security blanket wrapped around the entire field and are pushing toward your position from your left."

"Roger," Antonio responded. They waited just another five or so minutes as they saw the infrared strobes on the side of the house.

Max and Antonio led the way for their team to the side of the house, set up the makeshift ladder, and climbed to the roof. While doing this, Marco and his team moved to set up their breach on the front door. Once the team was on top, they flowed silently to the only door accessible to the rest of the house by the roof.

"Nate, there has to be a secret way to access that helo from inside the house. Alejandro has a safe room on the top floor in his master bedroom. I don't see any hatches up here, but I'm also not looking hard enough so keep a taut watch."

"I'm on it, don't worry."

Bypassing the helicopter sitting nestled on the pad, the team lined up to the right as they waited for the execute order to come from the team below. Max was amazed by the view. Although it was incredibly dark outside, the full moon illuminated the massive valley and trees below. It was an incredible sight to behold; he could even make out the outline of the city of Cartagena off in the distance. It was no wonder why Alejandro picked this place to live.

"Blue team, standing by."

Antonio and his men were in front of Max and the rest of his team, and when the execute order came across all earpieces and headsets, it sounded like World War III had erupted down below. Max had to trust the other operators, focusing in on his current objective, as the door hinges were blown apart by a breaching shotgun and the train flowed into the darkness below.

CHAPTER 45

Jack froze in his tracks; how could he be so stupid as to not check behind him? He could have sworn he didn't hear anything going on.

"Raise your hands, nice and slowly, sir." A stern voice came from behind him. Jack did as he was told, not wanting to escalate this any further and cause any commotion that would cause the drivers of the van to see his position. He turned around. Although it was dark, he could make out a silhouette of someone in a bathrobe and house slippers.

"What the hell are you doing hopping over my fence?" the person in front of him said. His deep Texas drawl reminded Jack where he was, and people down here wasted no time in shooting trespassers. Standing only an inch or two taller than Jack, the man poked Jack's chest with his double-barreled shotgun.

"Sir, I promise you that will be the last time you do that. Now, I don't want to have to hurt you, but I will," Jack said. The man behind the barrel laughed a little bit.

"You really think you're in any position to make threats?" He said, raising the shotgun so that the barrel was now pointed directly in front of Jack's face. Although the silhouetted man thought that would be a great form of intimidation to raise the shotgun, he couldn't have been more wrong. It was now level with where Jack had raised his arms and that did nothing but help him.

In a fraction of a second, Jack sidestepped and ducked to his right while pushing and simultaneously gripping the barrel up and to his left with his left hand. In doing so he yanked the barrel forward. The man was knocked off balance and Jack delivered a nasty brachial stun to his throat with his right palm, blocking the blood flow to the brain and instantly causing the man to collapse. Catching him before his body hit the ground, Jack dragged him back around to the back door of the house, careful to make sure he didn't run into any other surprises. Laying him down on his outdoor patio chair, he disassembled the shotgun and placed it on the patio underneath him. Doing a quick look behind him, he realized how close of an encounter that was.

His adrenaline was now coursing through his veins as the caffeine from the coffee he drank did nothing but add to the adrenaline dump. If he was doubting his ability to stay awake, he definitely was now. Going back to his original spot, he pulled out his pistol and attached the suppressor to the barrel. The van was still there, and he could faintly see the cigarette smoke billowing out of the passenger side of the vehicle.

The front yard of the house he was standing beside had nothing but grass and a walkway that joined the driveway. Luckily, there was only one car parked in the driveway, not that that meant anything, since the man's family could be inside right now and could have very well dialed the police. Not wanting to stick around to see if they showed up, Jack crept straight down to the sidewalk with his pistol now at the low and ready position. Stopping directly behind the van, he looked behind him one more time, and not seeing anyone, knelt to look below the van. He could see the driver's feet.

Rising, he swung around the driver's side of the vehicle and surprised the driver with a strike to the back of the head with the butt of the gun, dropping him in an instant. Stepping over the man lying knocked out on the ground, he pointed his gun through the window at the man who was sitting in the other seat.

"*Manos*," Jack said, forcefully opening the door. In doing so, the cabin lights came on, illuminating a grotesque figure of a man. Tattoos covered every inch of skin, from his bald head to the cigarette-crusted fingertips. Of all the tattoos covering his body, one tattoo in particular stood out: the infamous Saint Bertrand behind his left ear. He wasn't just playing with matches—these sicarios were kerosene.

The sicario shot a quick look at the pistol sitting on the dash right in front of him. Raising his hands, Jack noticed his cell phone was on speaker.

"*Dame el telefono,*" Jack whispered, not wanting to cause a scene in the middle of the cul-de-sac. Still hidden from the street lights, it wouldn't take much for someone to piece together what was going on. The sicario looked at the phone, then at Jack, and then at the gun.

"*¡Dame el telefono, pronto!*" Jack said, more sternly this time. Telling a sicario to willfully hand over his cellphone was like talking to a two-year-old. The words were lost on deaf ears.

As if on cue, the sicario tossed the phone violently toward Jack and reached for the pistol at the same time, but he was too slow. Jack's two nine-millimeter rounds blew through the sicario's neck as the bullets ripped through the open window and into the grass on the other side. Jack watched the life drain away from the man whose soul he was sure had died a long time ago.

Checking once more, making sure no one was watching— even though he was certain someone heard the gun going off—he opened the back of the van, dragging and heaving the driver into the back. He found what looked like the makings of a cleanup crew to a crime scene: duct tape, black tarps, water, bleach, whatever chemicals that could be used to hide a body.

He duct taped his unconscious victim before he remembered that the cell phone was still on speakerphone. Glancing at the front seat, he reached for it. The caller ID said *Jefe*. Knowing that meant boss in Spanish, Jack knew it could only be one person on the other end of the line.

CHAPTER 46

The stairs leading down from the rooftop into the house were short and dumped into a narrow hallway with three different paths to choose from: straight, right or left.

"Shit, weren't the lights supposed to be out?" Asked Kwame.

"I guess this guy had a gas generator installed. Let's move, carefully," Antonio answered. No sooner had he said that, than two sicario's came running around the corner, but caught off guard by the tactical force standing in their way. Antonio and Kwame wasted no time sending rounds their way, eating through their chest, ripping their lungs and hearts apart as they slumped to the ground.

Max, being the last person down the stairs, only heard the muffled shots, then silence. Three seconds later, he was stepping over two dead bodies, reminding him just how much he needed to be fully aware of his surroundings. Despite the fact they had not encountered stiff resistance yet, the loud noises below and the occasional round that ricocheted through the bottom of the floor kept them in reality.

Once they reached the intersection, Antonio said, "I'll break off with Max and his people, the rest of you secure the top floor and work your way down." With the simple instructions, the rest of his men broke off from the stack while Antonio, Max, Kwame, Kyle, Alex, and Courtney continued to the right.

Antonio pushed to the left side of the hallway while Max matched him step for step on the right. The paintings scattered throughout the hallway were some of the most fascinating paintings Max had ever seen. He had no doubt in his mind Alejandro had access to some of the most exquisite paintings from around the world. Some were of people, some of valleys, and some were of Alejandro and his late uncle.

As the hallway curved to the right, Max could make out two individuals standing in front of a set of closed double doors with their rifles dangling at chest level. That Alejandro had all the money in the world but couldn't afford better training for his men for situations like this said just how stingy people were when they were thrusted into the realm of making billions of dollars. No matter how much money people made, it seemed that the lowest ones on the totem pole working for the billionaires, always got stuck with the worst of services.

Max and Antonio sighted in and squeezed. Both guards took rounds to the chest and face this time. Dropping like a sack of potatoes, the inertia from the rounds slammed them against the door behind them. Walking up to them, Max kicked the bodies to the side as Antonio tried the doorknob.

"It's locked. Step back," Antonio said. Slinging his rifle to the right and replacing it with the small breaching shotgun slung across his left, he took aim at the door hinges. The doors nearly blew backward into the bedroom as the weapon dismantled them permanently. In the time it took Antonio to switch back to his rifle, Max had grabbed one of the flashbangs on his kit, pulled the pin, and let it fly through the threshold.

"Flashbang out!" he said through his throat mic, turning his head, along with the rest of the team. He waited until he heard the bang before pushing through, kicking whatever remnants of the door out of the way. The bedroom was massive. The first piece of furniture Max encountered was a large dresser at the front of the room with a number of watches, rings, and other jewelry. Above it sat a large television, which now had a massive crack in it from the concussive blast. In the center of the room was a large king-sized bed. Similar to the hallway he had just left, there were beautiful paintings but this time of naked women and fancy old school vehicles hanging on the walls.

As the group flowed into the room, Max banked hard right, followed by Kyle and Antonio, as Courtney and Kwame pushed left and Alex picked up the rear. Clearing the bedroom and bathroom, the team waited for Kwame and Courtney to clear the closet.

"Where is he?" Max asked Antonio, walking back outside the bathroom into the bedroom. Just as Antonio was about to respond, the team was interrupted by chatter on the line.

"Max...," the voice said.

"Nate, Nate, I can barely hear you," Max said, walking toward the window.

"Men... roof..."

"Say again, Nate. Dammit!" Max exclaimed, who felt like his heart was about to explode through his chest.

"I couldn't hear him either," Antonio said.

"These stupid radios are useless. I think Nate mentioned something about men on the roof."

"That's all I heard," Antonio replied, trying to reach one of his teammates on his own headset. The rest of the team ransacked the closet looking for anything resembling a hidden compartment. The closet was big enough to fit a full tactical team comfortably, which was astounding. Alejandro had so many nice clothes—but the team didn't care, the only thing on their mind was finding Ben. Shirts, business suits, slacks—you name it—were tossed onto the floor as they searched every inch.

Realizing he couldn't reach his team downstairs, Antonio ran over to the closet.

"Move!" Antonio shouted, "I've been here too many times." Pushing Alex practically to the ground. Walking up to the right wall, shoving a pair of Hugo Boss suits to the ground and exposing a large steel door, Antonio reached into his pocket and pulled out a small device. The device had a screen and as he held it to the digital keypad, they instantly synced with each other, as numbers flew across the screen.

"What's that?" Courtney asked, who knelt down beside him.

"Last year there was a series of bank robberies where they used this exact device to break into the bank vaults at night. You just place it against whatever keypad you're trying to open, and in a matter of seconds—" They heard a small click and a rotating of gears. "*Voila!*" Antonio said, as they both quickly stood up and stepped back.

Max pulled out his pistol and pointed it in the direction of the opening while reaching into his pocket and pulling out a second flashbang. Ripping the pin off, he said, "Ben is going to hate me for this but—" And then through the small space provided, he tossed it into the room and waited.

CHAPTER 47

Just before the shooting erupted, Pablo returned and locked himself with Ben and his boss in the safe room. When Alejandro heard the unmistakable sounds of rounds through the phone, he knew something was off. Quickly, Alejandro shut the phone down and shot Ben a glaring look.

Alejandro had called the Colombian Army ten minutes ago, but he knew it was going to take some time to get up their hill and knock out any resistance. He was screwed unless he could make it to his helicopter on the roof. Instructing Pablo to climb up the ladder and open the hatch above him he said, "You know what to do when you get up there."

Pushing the hatch up and hearing a loud clank on the other end as it bounced onto the cement, Pedro popped his head out. Not seeing anything, he signaled for Ben and Alejandro to make the climb to the top of the roof. It didn't take long for their eyes to adjust to the darkness, although the full moon helped.

Once they ascended the ladder, Alejandro ushered Ben toward the helicopter as Pablo hopped into the driver's seat and pressed a number of buttons and switches on the instrument panel.

Nate, not wanting to shoot the wrong person, tried to call it in but wasn't getting a response.

"Fuck! I hate these radios," he said. "Do you guys have a signal?"

"Amigo, I can't get through either," one of the men lying on the ground next to him said.

"I'm not taking the shot 'cause I don't want to hit what possibly might be our boy," Nate said, cursing under his breath. All he could make out from the ridge with the thermal scope were three figures on the roof. Even though the men were energizing the helicopter, the last thing he wanted to do was come all this way to shoot Ben. Making the shot wasn't the hard part, not being able to have someone properly identify the targets was.

Entering the safe room and clearing it, Max cursed again under his breath. "Where is he?"

"The ladder!" Antonio said, pointing up to the ceiling.

"We doing this?" Kwame asked, poking his head into the small room, not wanting to take up too much space. "I may need help getting through that hatch."

"Do we have a choice?" Kyle asked, looking up. Just then the whining of an engine grew louder above them.

"Enough chat, let's go!" Max screamed. "I didn't come all this way to get this close and let him slip through our grasp again."

"Nate, come in," Courtney said, but there was no response.

Max was first to ascend the ladder, and once he reached the top, he slung the hatch open. Waiting just below the top for any incoming fire, which never came, he grabbed his pistol in his right hand while using his left to launch himself up off the ladder and onto the rooftop. The helicopter, which was facing the opposite direction, appeared at first glance to be an old school Huey, clearly restored to look brand new. Not seeing anyone else on the roof, Max assumed everyone was inside the helicopter. Max knelt and tried to reach Nate now that he was outside.

"Nate, come in," he said.

"Finally! Where have y'all been? There are three guys inside of that helo but I can't positively ID any of them, so I didn't take the shots."

Barely being able to hear him through the earpiece because of the engines roaring, Max yelled, "You're certain there's only three?"

"Unless whoever is in that bird can do magic and make more people appear, yes. I've had my eyes glued to this roof ever since y'all breached," he said. "What would you like me to do?"

The group was on the roof now and watching the blades spin at full throttle approximately fifteen yards ahead of them. The noise from the turbo whine and full rotation of the blades was unbearable to everyone except for Antonio, whose headset was also noise cancelling. Chatter on comms was virtually non-existent now, so the use of signs was the group's best option.

Max signaled for them to take a knee and ran to the other edge of the roof to try and finish his communication with Nate. "Alejandro isn't going to be flying his own bird!" Max yelled, "Aim for the pilot!"

"Roger." Taking aim at the pilot, and slowing his breathing, Nate pulled the trigger, sending one round directly in front of the cockpit. "Dammit," he cursed, adjusting his sights. Doing his best to slow his breath again, he took another shot that broke glass right above the pilot's head.

Hearing the round and glass shatter, but not seeing the helicopter drop to the deck, Kyle assumed the obvious as he turned to Kwame. "Someone has to go to the range when we get back," he yelled. Kwame just gave him a blank stare, pointing to his ear and shaking his head. Kyle nodded, pointed at Nate's position and laughed, shaking his own head. Kwame returned his laugh with a blank stare and a shaking of his head.

The team watched in suspense as the helicopter gained altitude. Nate took a third shot through the pilot house. The helicopter slammed back down onto the deck, and as it smacked the roof hard, smoke billowed from the engine as the rotors started whining down.

"Tango down! She's all yours!" Nate said, watching the pilot slump over.

"Let's go!"

The stack split into two groups, each taking a side and treading lightly toward the helicopter. Just then the door on right swung open as two people stumbled out.

"You came a long way to rescue your friend!" Alejandro shouted, managing to stumble out of the helicopter behind Ben with the assault rifle pointed at his back. "Unless you all just came to arrest me? But if that's the case, then you are sadly mistaken because I will never die out here! This is *my* country!"

"Drop the gun, Alejandro, you've got no place to go!" Max shouted. Kwame and Kyle were lined up next to him, but neither one of them could get a clear shot. Antonio, Courtney, and Alex managed to wrap their way around the left side of the helicopter without being detected. As the team moved down the side approaching the cockpit, Antonio sent two more rounds into Pablo's chest when he created a feeble attempt to point his pistol in their direction when they walked by.

"Tango down, officially," Antonio said.

"Come out from that side!" Alejandro said, adjusting his stance and backing up to the edge of the roof. Ben's arms were down by his side, trying to maintain his balance as the leader of the Saint Bertrand Cartel gripped the back of his shirt, using him as a human shield.

"How are you doing, Ben?" shouted Courtney, emerging with the rest of her group from the other side of the helicopter.

"Oh, you know me, just hanging out."

"*Callate!*" screamed Alejandro. "You all wrecked my fields, my submarines, and now my house is destroyed! I run this country! What do you think will happen if you arrest me? Do you hear those sirens in the distance?" He paused, noticing a couple of members cocking his head to the left, listening to the raging sounds of sirens off in the distance.

"You're dreaming if you think I'm going to let you walk out of this," Antonio exclaimed, tightening his grip on the rifle. The group managed to formed a *U*-shape around Alejandro and Ben, who were backed up to the edge with nothing but the veranda beneath.

"Nate, do you have a shot?" Kwame asked, as softly as he could.

"Negative, y'all are standing on the other side of the helicopter, big boy."

"I'll tell you what you're going to do," Alejandro said.

"Enlighten me," Antonio said, trying to sight in on Alejandro's head.

"You're going to let me and your beloved Ben here walk through you, down the side ladder, and into one of my—"

Just then two rounds shot up from below and through both of Alejandro's shoulder blades, causing him to drop the rifle and fall to his knees. Hearing the rifle hit the deck behind him, Ben turned around and kicked the rifle away, sending it off the roof.

Watching Alejandro on his knees not being able to move either arm, Ben cold-cocked him in the face, sending blood and mucous all over the deck. As Kyle and Kwame subdued Alejandro, the rest of the team ran up and lowered weapons. Courtney was the first one to give Ben a hug.

"Don't shoot, peeking over the edge," Antonio said into the headset. He saw Marco and a couple of men wave to him from the veranda, and he waved back. As Antonio talked to Marco and tried to figure out the ex-fill strategy, the rest of the Bering group gave Ben hugs and handshakes. Max was the last one to walk up.

"Who are you?" Ben asked, sitting down as Courtney checked his vitals.

"Just a distant friend," he said, extending his hand. "Welcome back."

Ben took it and looked at Alex. "Don't worry, man, we'll have plenty of time to fill you in on the ride back," Alex said.

Antonio walked back over to the rest of the group, "Okay, lady and gents, we have to leave now. I don't care how cool of a group you think you are, but we don't want to be here if the army gets here."

"What about this guy?" Kyle asked, pointing to Alejandro, who was screaming in pain from his bullet-ridden arms cuffed behind him.

"Oh, shut up," Antonio said, kicking him hard in the chest, sending him on his back. Alejandro let out a small yelp as tears flowed down both cheeks. Antonio felt no remorse as he leaned over and said, "Say hi to Saint Bertrand for me, *pendejo*." Pulling his pistol out, he sent a single round through his skull, the noise piercing the night sky.

The shot surprised the team, especially Kyle, who was standing right next to him when he shot. Walking up to Antonio, Max smirked.

"Here I was thinking you were going to let him live."

"Fuck this *puto*," Antonio replied, spitting on his corpse.

Scratching his beard, Max replied, "That also works." Covering the mic, he leaned into Antonio. "Have you made a decision yet?"

Covering his own lapel mic and turning his head to look Max right in the eye, he responded, "What kind of rifles do we get to use?"

CHAPTER 48

Twenty-four hours later, the Gulfstream G550 ordered by Janet to pick up the group, landed with a soft thump onto the runway as the screaming engines reversed throttle and slowed. Max woke from his deep sleep and saw that he was the last person to wake up and stretch, rotating his neck and shoulders to loosen up his stiff body. Looking around, it was as if nothing ever happened. The atmosphere was euphoric, everyone joking and smiling, not being able to wait to get home.

He was glad the team was functioning at full strength, but more importantly, he completed what he said he was going to for his old partner and friend. As the plane taxied to the hangar, he saw his bright red Porsche through the window parked right where he left it. Rubbing his eyes and using the lever below him to move the seat forward, he sat up and stretched once more. Alex was sitting next to him reading an article on his iPad when he leaned over to Max. "Welcome back to lovely Virginia, the most boring state in the world."

Chuckling, Max said, "Where are you from?"

"The great state of New Mexico," answered Alex.

"Not bad, not bad. Why do you hate it here?" Max asked, clearing his throat, still looking out of the window as his Porsche disappeared from view and was replaced with the interior of the hangar.

Leaning back in his chair and turning off his iPad, he responded, "Honestly, this area isn't bad. I just don't like that the military is everywhere. Besides camping there's really nothing to do here. It's nothing but strip malls and people with ridiculous vanity plates."

Laughing some more, Max replied, "I'm not going to argue you

on that one. Being from Cali, this is definitely a change of pace."
After the plane came to a stop, the pilots lowered the steps and
one by one the operators left the cabin. Max made sure he was the
last one to leave. He looked back at the empty cabin, he thought
to himself, yeah, he could definitely use a change of pace. After
all, more time at home meant he could finally ask the redhead at
the pub out on a date. Catching a glimpse of the digital clock from
the open cockpit, he saw it was just past four o'clock, which meant
there was still time to head to the pub to catch happy hour.

Reaching the bottom of the stairs, he noticed everyone else heading to their cars, wasting no time at all to get home. He couldn't wait
to have that first beer touch his lips, and maybe talk to Samantha if
she was working. Walking down the stairs and rounding the corner
outside of the hangar, he saw a very familiar face.

"If it isn't the great killer himself," Jack said, leaning onto
Max's Porsche and holding out his hand. Max shook his head
and continued walking to the hood of his car. Setting his bag on
the ground, he pulled out his key fob, and opened the hood, and
noticed a bright yellow Corvette C8 parked next to him.

"Why do you need a Corvette? Are you in a midlife crisis?"
Max asked, placing his bag inside.

"You're a funny guy. Just let me know when you want to line
them up and we'll see who gets the last laugh."

"Yeah, okay bud," Max said, Max motioning for his friend to
stop leaning on his paint job, and shut the hood.

"Have you given what I asked you any more thought? We could
definitely use you."

"I know you didn't drive to the airport to ask me a question
that you could have just called for. What is it this time?"

"You do know me all too well. I have one more thing that
needs wrapping up. I promise this is the last favor I ask," Jack said,
adjusting his RayBan's.

"I've heard that one before," he said, opening the driver's door and pausing.

Reaching behind his back, Jack pulled out an envelope but as he was about to hand it over, he pulled it back. "Are you going to work for me or not?"

"If you ask me again, I might change my mind," Max responded.

"That's the Max I know," Jack said, handing him the envelope. He watched him open it and read the contents.

"Are you sure about this?"

"Absolutely, it's already been cleared."

"By whom?"

"Why do you ask so many questions?" Jack replied, shooting him a quick wink.

"Okay, then," Max said, "consider it done."

The two friends shook hands and then Max jumped in, backed up, and peeled off toward the exit.

He stopped home only to park and drop his bag off. Entering the Irish pub, he didn't see the red-headed girl of his dreams working, but nonetheless, he exhausted and was just elated to be back. Finishing his first beer and about to grab his second, he heard a familiar voice next to him.

"Is this seat taken?"

Snapping his head to the right, he saw Courtney, and boy did she clean up nicely. Wearing skin-tight blue jeans, a long-sleeved button-down shirt with the top couple of buttons undone, and her long blonde hair relaxed, touching her waist, she took a seat. Her bright blue eyes stared into his. He was speechless.

"You look like you just saw a ghost, man," she said, smiling and putting her wallet and keys on the bar top.

"What are you doing here?" he asked, surprised.

"What does anyone do at an Irish pub?" she said. "To have a drink! Let's get a shot or two in before I answer that question."

EPILOGUE

Alexandria loved to go on boat rides when friends invited her, and she had a lot of friends with boats. Growing up around them because her father loved to fish, she developed a passion for them, but she was more of the partying type. It wasn't until college that she got her first taste of partying on expensive yachts, thanks to her ability to woo almost any guy she wanted to. That knack she had for being in control followed her well into her job working for the CIA. It also helped her accomplish her side job of making money by selling secrets and making back door deals with shady people. She was also frugal, and was taught at a young age how important it was to save money for important items.

Her plan was, as soon as she saved enough money, she was going to move out of the city, buy a house somewhere in Virginia, and make the short commute to work.

It had been about a week since she made her last cell phone call to Pablo, and she hadn't heard from him since. No matter, she was going on vacation now, and if they needed more work or something else, they would definitely give her a call.

When Jack handed Max the envelope at the airport, he felt no remorse. Hacking Alexandria's computer and acquiring her trip itinerary was the easy part—Jack had Preston do that for him. No, the hard part, believe it or not, was trying to find a last-minute flight to Key West the same time she was headed down there. But he accomplished it.

After Max checked into his hotel, he drove the rental car around the small island and looked for quick evacuation routes—not that it was this kind of mission, but he was a creature of habit. Booking a flight ahead of his target allowed him to spot her and follow her the second her plane touched down.

Alexandria's best friend from college lived in the Keys and invited her out to accompany her on her boyfriend's boat. Taking the next week off and scrubbing whatever plans she had, she grabbed the next flight out. Her friend was waiting for her at the airport, greeting her and reminiscing on everything over the past couple of years. It had been a while since they had seen each other.

Due to the nature of her job, it had been a while since Alexandria had sex with a decent-looking man; she was so busy selling herself for information that she hadn't really had time to date, but tonight she was on the prowl.

As both girls threw on their best cocktail dresses, her best friend called up some more girlfriends and the small group of attractive women hit Duval Street, which was littered with more bars and restaurants than a person could count. Your typical Friday in Key West meant the bars, clubs, and streets were packed full of people. This also made it that much easier for Max to complete his tasking.

It was late evening now as Max sat in his car off the main strip. He let Alexandria get nice and intoxicated for a couple of hours before he made his move. Walking through the alleyway connected to the parking lot which dumped out onto the main strip, he checked his phone and saw that his target was already inside. In addition to hacking into her computer, he had Preston introduce a bug remotely onto her phone that showed Max her location at all times. It was too easy.

Wearing shorts, a short-sleeved shirt, and a weathered Dodgers ball cap, he looked like every other person just wanting to get a quick drink at a dive bar. Showing his fake driver's license to the security guard, he made his way through the crowd and right up to the bar. He ordered a beer and pretended to care about the football game being shown across all of the monitors.

Looking to his right, he spotted his target and her four friends who were only thirty feet or so away. They were all running low on drinks. Quickly scanning the entire bar, and looking for his way in, he found it.

Sitting closer to the entrance were five guys young guys who seemed to be well into the night with their empty beer bottles stacked upside down inside of the bucket on the table. The hooting and hollering coming from their table only added to the allure of using them as his scapegoats. He ordered four Mojito's and one tequila sunrise, and after the bartender to put them together, he reached into his pocket and pulled out two small pills.

The active ingredient in eye drops is a chemical called tetrahydrozoline, and when induced the proper way into the eyes, it helped to narrow the blood vessels causing the redness in the eyes to subside. However, when introduced to the digestive tract, it was known to be lethal in many cases. One pill of the main ingredient was more than enough to send its victim to the hospital. However, he needed to be certain and the last thing he wanted was to use his pistol—that could get messy. Besides, a lot of the people who didn't look like much working at the agency knew a decent amount of self-defense. Max was in no condition to get into another fist fight after what he just experienced the last week, so he chose the easy way out.

As drinks were brought to him, he handed the bartender his credit card. As he turned around to insert it into the machine, Max used his right hand to reach over the drinks to grab some napkins and simultaneously dropped both pills in the tequila sunrise. In the fifteen seconds it took for the bartender to turn around and hand him his card back, there was nothing to be seen inside the drink other than the beautiful bright red-orange and yellow colors of the cocktail.

Taking a shot of tequila and slamming it back onto the counter, he noticed a waiter walk up next to him about to order a set of drinks.

"Hey man," Max said, tapping the younger gentleman on the shoulder.

Greeting him with a smile, he said, "Yes, sir, how can I help you?"

"You see those gentlemen over there?" he asked, pointing to the howling men in their colorful shirts, shorts, and boat shoes.

"Yes, sir, I do," responded the waiter.

"We're all down here on vacation, but unfortunately I have to leave. I'm not feeling too well, but they find those women standing over there very attractive," he said pointing to Alexandria's group. "Can you make sure you get these drinks to them? My friends are a little shy, so I think this will break the ice."

Laughing, he responded, "Of course!"

"Great! Thanks, man. By the way I think I saw the redhead drinking the sunrise earlier, so that's for her. Just tell them the drinks are from them, not me," he said, slipping a twenty-dollar bill into the breast pocket of the man's Hawaiian shirt.

Noticing his generous tip, the waiter nodded, grabbed a drink tray, set the drinks on top, and was off. Quickly walking to another corner of the bar but making sure he was still in eyesight of the drinks being delivered, he made sure that Alexandria got her drink. She did.

After watching her take a few sips, he was satisfied that she would drink the entire cocktail. He made his way through the crowd and back onto the street. Wandering across the road full of potholes and cracks from the constant battering of hurricanes, he entered another bar and ordered a beer and a burger. He sat outside in silence to enjoy his late-night snack. This was the boring part, but he had to make sure the job was one-hundred percent complete. He couldn't afford to let Jack down.

Two hours dragged by and his target was still inside. He wondered if the drugs had worked. At this point all he wanted to do was get back to the hotel and go to sleep. As if on cue, not five minutes later the girls stumbled outside with the men who were sitting by the entrance. Watching the group laugh—and seeing that some of the men were probably going to get lucky based on their body language—he kept his eyes fixated on Alexandria. She was now swaying heavily and had to use a nearby light pole to lean on in an effort to keep her balance. Smiling, he took a sip of his Corona and watched as she instantly dropped to the concrete, completely lifeless. Listening as the crowd gathered, he heard someone lean over and touch her neck. "She has no pulse!"

His job was complete. With two lethal doses, it had worked its way into her digestive system by now, soaked into the walls of her intestines, and from there moved into her blood stream. The drug, when exposed to the heart, caused it to either beat too fast or too slow, depending on the person. After walking back to his vehicle, he drove back to the hotel to get some sleep and looked forward to the early flight back to D.C. in the morning.

CPSIA information can be obtained
at www.ICGtesting.com
Printed in the USA
LVHW102343040422
715272LV00015B/287/J